shattered

Gianna Emiko Barnes

Fulton Books, Inc.
Meadville, PA

Published by Fulton Books 2021

ISBN 978-1-63710-769-0 (paperback)
ISBN 978-1-63710-770-6 (digital)

Printed in the United States of America

PROLOGUE

What the fuck am I doing? Taryn thought to herself as she stood in line to get on a red-eye and head back to Hawai'i. She felt absolutely stupid for dropping her life, leaving her family, and running home to help a man that pretty much destroyed her entire world. But she knew why she was running, and Toby's pleas were merely an excuse to run away from San Francisco. To run away from Derek. She didn't know if the accusations she made in the letter to him were accurate or not, but she was sure of what she saw. Him kissing his ex, Lexie, after emphasizing to Taryn how special she was to him and how he was developing feelings for her. She should've known it was too good to be true. They had known each other for less than a week, and Lexie was his high school sweetheart. History trumps fling every time. But that didn't make what happened hurt any less than it did.

Taryn was strong though, and over the years, dealing with endless losses in her life, she knew how to compartmentalize her emotions, often using reason and logic to push herself forward and take the necessary next steps in her life. She wasn't about to let Derek start clouding her judgment now. Her focus had to be on Toby. She had this flight, give or take twenty-four hours, to get her mind right and gather up the courage to face his family, aside from his mother, who still thought Taryn had just left Toby because she wanted to be single again. But for the life of her, no matter how strong and tough she had to be facing difficult situations in the past, this hit her differently. She hated lying and being fake to people, but that's exactly what she had to do now—play along with the story they fed to Toby's other family members so she could follow through on his mother's request to see her one last time. His mother was an amazing woman, and to this day, Taryn would do anything for her.

The call Toby had made to her earlier that evening shattered her world. Never could Taryn ever imagine him calling her again, let alone call her, begging for her to come and help him. But she wasn't doing this for Toby. She was doing this for his mother, Trisha. When Toby called, he somberly shared that his mother was very sick. Earlier that week, her doctors hospitalized her for her ongoing illness, ran more tests, and diagnosed her with stage 4 cancer from a brain tumor. A small growth they had been watching for years that embedded itself in her brain, suddenly spread like wildfire. The doctors gave her a mere week left to live.

That's when Toby called Taryn. It was his by his mother's request to see her, one last time, before she passed. Although Taryn had remained close to Toby's mom, helping her whenever she reached out, being an ear for her to vent to, Taryn didn't think her relationship with her former mother-in-law was that significant to anyone else. But if Toby's mom really needed to see Taryn before she passed, who was Taryn to deny her that? For Trisha, Taryn could deal with facing the hate from Toby's family, just for one day.

1

Taryn

"We will now begin boarding all first-class passengers." The flight attendant's voice rang out over the airport speakers.

Taryn walked up to the check-in stand and handed her ticket to the attendant with a smile.

"Thank you," she said as she took her ticket back and headed down the jetway." She took a deep breath and clenched her eyes, the jet fuel filling her nose. The cold night air could be felt through the thin jetway walls and were like daggers piercing through her jacket. As Taryn entered the plane, she showed another attendant her ticket as he escorted her to her window seat in the last row of first class.

"Let me help you with your bag, ma'am," he said with a smile as he took Taryn's roller carry-on and lifted it as if it were weightless, placing it in the overhead bin above her seat. "Can I start you with a drink?"

"God, yes!" Taryn sighed as she dropped her purse onto the aisle seat next to hers and plopped down. "Cranberry vodka, please?"

"Of course," he said with a smile, trying to hold in his laughter at Taryn's eagerness for some alcohol.

"Thank you." Taryn smiled.

Shuffling through her bag, Taryn took out her phone and charger as she started to settle into her seat. She left her bag on the seat next to hers. She made sure to book it so no one else could sit next to her and she could be alone with her thoughts.

"Ti?" Kyle's voice pulled her from digging into her bag.

"Kyle? Tyson?" she questioned as the two men stopped at the seats across the aisle from hers. "I thought you weren't heading home until Friday?"

"That's what we thought too," Tyson started sarcastically. "But dummy over here only checked the dates, not the actual days he booked the flights, and the dates he looked at to come home were based on the days of the week for June!" he added angrily, looking over his shoulder at Kyle.

"Hey, in my defense, I told you I'm not good at booking crap. I don't have the patience," he retorted. "And I was also stoned," he whispered with a chuckle.

"See what I have to deal with?" Tyson griped. "Between this one and your boy Lewis, I'm surprised I haven't ended up in a mental institution yet!" he joked.

"Wait, why are you here? I thought you told Lewie-boy you staying in the Bay until Sunday?" Kyle asked.

"Yeah, something came up, and I had to take the next flight out," Taryn said with a heavy sigh.

"Must've been bad if you had to leave. Where're your parents?" Kyle continued.

"They're still with my brother." Taryn forced a smile.

"If it's so bad, why aren't they going home too?" Tyson asked suspiciously.

Tears began to well in Taryn's eyes. First, what happened with Derek, then Toby calling, and now she had to face interrogation when her emotions were barely in check. Taryn began taking deep breaths to try and calm herself before answering as Tyson and Kyle stared at her.

"Here's your cranberry vodka, ma'am," the flight attendant said as he handed her the drink. "Please let me know if you need anything else."

"Thank you," Taryn said with a tear-filled smile.

He took his cue to leave, and the attendant walked away before turning and throwing a concerned glance toward Taryn.

"Same old Ti. The second you're upset, the whole world wants to come save you," Kyle teased.

"What?" Taryn questioned as she took a large swig of her drink.

"Nothing. So what happened?" Tyson asked casually as he went on his phone.

Kyle glanced over Tyson's shoulder with a frown before nodding and turning his attention to Taryn. She was so upset that she was oblivious to Tyson muting his phone while he called Lewis so he could listen in on their conversation. After a slight pause, Taryn spilled her guts to Kyle and Tyson in between sobs. Behind them, the rest of the plane continued to fill up as more people began to board.

"I'm sorry. I didn't mean to dump that all on you guys." Taryn sighed when she was finally done summing up what was going on with Toby and why she was going home. She made sure to leave Derek out of adding to her emotional instability. What was going on with Toby alone was too much for her brain to handle.

"It's okay. We got you, Ti," Kyle said with a smile.

"Yes, we do, and I'm sure Lewis would have your back too. You should call him and talk to him for support before you head to the hospital," Tyson stated.

"I know. He got upset with me when I didn't call him for support during my divorce, and I could honestly use an old friend right now," she said, smiling, as she wiped away her tears.

"Sir, you need to hang up your phone and put it on airplane mode please," the attendant said as he went down the aisle to do a final check of everything before takeoff.

"Oh, sorry. I didn't know it was on." Tyson tried to play it off. "Gotta go, bro. Bye," he whispered into the phone before hanging up.

"Who was that?" Taryn questioned.

"Lewis, duh," Kyle stated matter-of-factly.

Taryn's heart sank at the thought of Lewis hearing her conversation over the phone. Just then, her phone buzzed on her lap. She knew it wasn't Derek because she had muted her conversation with him. She sighed as Lewis's name flashed on her screen, and she opened the message.

"Call me when you land. Love you lots Ti. I got you." (Lewis)

Turning her phone to airplane mode, Taryn tucked it back into her bag. Letting out a heavy sigh, she relaxed back into her seat, trying to enjoy some final moments of peace before landing in the chaos awaiting her in Hawai'i.

*****

"Ti, wake up." Tyson gently shook her as the plane taxied in from landing. "We're home."

"Thanks," Taryn said, rubbing the sleep from her eyes.

"Yo, you knocked the fuck out last night," Kyle teased. "Still the same old Ti. Vodka kicking you in the ass, huh?"

"OMG, you're so loud," Taryn said as she began to gather her things.

"Come on. We'll help you get your bags and stuff," Tyson said, bringing her carry-on down from the overhead bin as the plane parked and the seat belt light turned off.

"Yeah, Lewis'll kick our asses if we don't take care of you right now," Kyle confessed.

"Guys, I'm fine," Taryn tried to convince them as they exited the plane and headed for baggage claim.

"You don't got a choice. We're dropping you off at home too," Tyson said with finalization in his tone.

All Taryn could do was sigh and follow them. She was appreciative of all their support but couldn't help but feel like a burden.

The heat of the Hawai'i air sucker punched Taryn in the face as she could feel sweat start to form at the base of her neck even at 4:00 a.m. It was hot, but she was home and glad to be there. Taking a deep breath, she could smell the hint of saltwater in the air and smiled despite herself.

Everything from there seemed to go in slow motion. The guys grabbed her suitcase and carry-on for her, and they piled into Kyle's beat-up van that he left parked at the airport. The drive on the small crowded freeway nearly put her back to sleep, but she smiled as she watched the familiar landmarks pass her window as they headed toward Wai'anae.

After passing the bustling city of Kapolei, the van took the bend around a mountain as her hometown came into view. The stretch of white sand and green palm trees lined the road to one side, with tall green mountains on the other. The blue sky seemed to smile down on her. She was glad that she was home as the rich blueness of the ocean glistened against the rays of the sun. They drove along a few miles more, and they finally pulled up to her house.

"Thanks, you guys, for everything. I'm impressed you remember where I lived," Taryn said with a grateful smile.

"Hey, we were here how many times a week to sneak you out after midnight when you were back in high school," Tyson joked.

"Yeah, before Tyson became an old man," Kyle added.

The three of them laughed as Taryn climbed out. Tyson helped get her bags out of the back before giving her a hug.

"Just call us if you need anything, okay? We got you, Ti," Tyson said as he got back into the van.

"Thank you guys again. Get home safely!" Taryn said with a smile before punching in the code to the key box by her garage door.

As she entered the house, the familiar smell of home comforted her. She dropped her bags in the foyer. The strength she exuded fell away as the emptiness of her house overwhelmed her. Her emotions suddenly took control of her as she collapsed to her knees and sobbed.

2

Nathan

It was barely 6:00 a.m. in San Francisco, but Nathan was already up. He couldn't sleep much last night after Taryn had left. Checking his phone again, he still had not heard from her, and he wanted to talk to her first before he told his parents what was going on.

Unable to just lay there anymore, Nathan threw on sweatpants, a jacket, and running shoes and headed out the door. Reaching the bottom of the steps to their building, he noticed Derek's car still parked across the street.

Did this guy really sleep here to wait for Ti? Nathan thought as he crossed the street carefully, heading over to Derek's car. He knocked on the window, and Derek shot up in the driver's seat.

"Nathan?" he said sleepily as he rolled down the window, pulling a jacket up over his chest like a blanket.

"Did you sleep here all night?" Nathan asked.

"Yeah, I'm just waiting for Taryn. I need to talk to her, and I think she blocked my number on her phone. It goes straight to voice mail when I call now, and all my messages were left unread," Derek said, his eyes swollen from crying.

"Well, you're going to be waiting a while," Nathan said with a sigh. "She left."

The words shot life through Derek as he flew the door open and got out of the car, forcing Nathan to step backward.

"What? What do you mean she left?" Derek asked, confused. He slammed his door behind him.

"She left. Exactly what I said," Nathan repeated. "We came home from getting crepes last night, and I found a letter on the counter from her. She took a red-eye back to Hawai'i last night."

Derek collapsed against his car. His mouth went agape in disbelief. Her running away from him, all the way back to Hawai'i confirmed that he had lost her forever. There was no coming back from this. He had fucked up beyond repair. Seeing Derek so distraught, Nathan began to feel bad for him, realizing that his feelings for his sister was deeper than he could have imagined. Taryn had mentioned in her letter that it wouldn't work between the two of them, but something bigger must have happened for Derek to react the way he did, and Nathan was suddenly torn between having empathy for Derek and protecting his sister.

"Do you want to grab some coffee?" Nathan asked empathetically. "I need some, and you look like it could definitely help right now."

Derek nodded, locked his car, and followed Nathan down the sidewalk and around the block to the coffee shop. After getting two cups of black coffee, they sat down at a table just outside.

"So what happened?" Nathan asked vaguely, seeing if he could squeeze some insight into whatever mental breakdown his sister had last night.

"I fucked up, Nate." Derek sighed, sipping the hot liquid.

"Well, obviously." Nathan scoffed, motioning at Derek's physical state.

"Ti was supposed to meet me on the set of my show because we started filming yesterday, and I was running late. The Uber I sent for her got her to the set, security escorted her in to my trailer, and then...hurricane Lexie hit," Derek began with a heavy sigh.

Taking a sip of his coffee, Nathan leaned back and nodded for Derek to continue.

"Lexie is my ex," Derek said with guilt-ridden eyes. "She's getting married this weekend, and she showed up on set with a visitor's pass from one of our social media marketers and kissed me. She wanted one last fling before she got married." Derek's head dropped as he clenched the cup of coffee for dear life, his forearms resting on the edge of the wooden table.

"I'm guessing Ti was there and saw everything?" Nathan suggested, confirming there was more to her mental breakdown than just Toby calling her. His sister had her heart broken again before it was even fixed and was running before giving Derek a chance to explain.

"Yes," Derek said on a heavy sigh. "I stopped it though, the kiss, and had security remove her from the premises. But I guess it was too late. Taryn was already gone."

"This is why I told her not to jump into anything too soon. I knew that her heart wasn't ready for an upset again, even if it sounds like it was just a huge misunderstanding," Nathan tried to reason. "But you weren't the only reason she ran, so don't beat yourself up too much. Seeing the kiss probably triggered her memories of being cheated on and crap, but I think the call from Toby sent her over the edge."

"Toby called her? Her ex-husband Toby?" Derek asked, stunned.

"Yeah. She noted it in the letter but didn't say anything more than she had to go home to help him, that he needed her or some bullshit." Nathan rolled his eyes. "She was always too nice. Her heart breaks so hard all the time because it's just way too big. She's too fucking nice."

Derek sat back, his mind clearly racing as his eyes radically moved around in his head. He took another swig of his coffee. Placing his cup down, Nathan leaned forward and gave Derek a hard look.

"I know you care about Ti, but I think you just need to let her go. Walk away before either of you fall any harder and end up hurting each other worse than you already have. This is so much drama already, and it hasn't been a week!" Nathan stated with frustration.

"Has she called you or texted you?" Derek asked, completely ignoring Nathan's request.

"No. The letter was the last I heard from her," Nathan replied with a sigh. "She should be landing soon, though, if she took the red-eye home."

"Okay." Derek nodded. "Please tell her I got her letter and she was wrong. That I feel the same way she does."

"I don't know, D. I'm not sure I can do that. She's already hurting. I don't want to set her up to get hurt anymore," Nathan said, feeling protective of his sister.

"Please," Derek pleaded. "Please."

3

Taryn

"Dr. Colliare to the ER. Paging Dr. Colliare to the ER." A nurse's voice could be heard over the speaker of the hospital.

Taryn felt like a robot, going through the motions as she moved down the white hallways of the hospital toward the elevators on Friday morning. The ICU where Trisha was at was on the second floor. The cold temperature of the building added to the coldness Taryn felt inside as she mentally tried to numb herself from the pain, preparing for what she was inevitably going to face in the next few minutes. Taking deep breaths, she tried to steady her heart as she got into the elevator. The smell of rubbing alcohol and rubber gloves filled her nose with discomfort.

Taryn clenched her eyes shut for one more moment of peace, and she held her breath as if trying to hold onto her sanity. *I shouldn't be here*, she thought as the elevator dinged, signifying she was at the ICU.

"You can do this, Ti. Just smile, stay quiet, and everything will be okay," she said to herself as she took a deep breath and stepped out of the elevator.

She felt a thousand eyes look up at her as she entered the ICU waiting room, piercing into her like daggers. Toby's entire family was here, from his aunts and uncles, to his cousins and their kids. The tension was extenuating. Taryn took a deep breath and walked forward with her head held high.

Annalee looked up from the corner nearest the ICU entrance doors. Her tan skin seemed pale, and her dark black hair looked dull from the stress she must have been going through with a new-born and dealing with Trisha's cancer. Not to mention, on the phone Toby shared they recently had a small ceremony a month ago to get married. Her petite frame looked frail like a piece of glass. Despite Annalee being the reason her own marriage fell apart, Taryn felt sorry for her.

"Taryn," Annalee said gently, getting up quickly and rushing over to a frozen Taryn who was suddenly halted at the entrance to the waiting room. Everyone's stares held her firmly in place. "Toby is already in there with his mom. She's not doing well. I'll take you to them."

All eyes were on Taryn and Annalee as they crossed the waiting room, yet no one said a single word to Taryn. Still, she kept a kind smile on her face and followed Annalee through the ICU doors.

"It's this first room here. They knew she had a big family, so they kept her as close to them as possible," Annalee explained as she knocked on the door and opened it.

The room was dark, with what little light there was peeking through the opened curtains. The beeping of the breathing machine was loud and seemed to echo in the tiny space. Trisha was hooked up to multiple tubes, and the glowing spirit she embodied seemed to have faded away. In one corner of the room, near the window, Toby's older brother, Talon, sat with his typical scowl on his face. Toby's dad Terrance sat next to Trisha, holding her hand on the edge of the bed. Toby, who was staring at his mother, was sitting at the foot of her bed. All three men looked exhausted as they turned their attention to Taryn and Annalee.

"You got some nerve showing your face here," Talon seethed, anger radiating through him suddenly as he stood up. "Who the fuck told you it was okay to come here after what you put our family through?"

"Talon, not here," Terrance scolded.

"No, Dad. She doesn't belong here. You're not fucking family anymore, Taryn. No one wants you here, so fucking leave," Talon said through his teeth, his hands clenched at his side.

"I wanted her here," Trisha said weakly, her voice breaking through the tension in the room, causing everyone to fall instantly silent.

Trisha had not spoken for three days. Everyone was stunned at her response. She reached a hand out to Taryn, and tears began to fill everyone's eyes. Some in sadness, others in anger. Taryn moved to her side and took her hand without question.

"Ti," Trisha said heavily. "I'm sorry," she continued as she squeezed Taryn's hand and a tear rolled from her eyes.

"Don't worry. It's water under the bridge. You just need to save that energy to get better, okay?" Taryn said gently, her voice breaking with sadness as tears welled in the corners of her eyes.

"Sorry? What the fuck are you apologizing to this bitch for, Mom?" Talon exploded.

"Shhhh! You're going to upset your mom, and everyone is going to hear you in the waiting room," Terrance said sternly.

"I don't fucking care! This selfish bitch came in and wrecked our family! If it weren't for Annalee, Toby would still be a fucking mess!" Talon raged on. "If anyone owes someone an apology in this room, it's you, Taryn! You fucking self—" Talon didn't get to finish.

"It's not her fault!" Toby interrupted his brother, unable to just sit there and let Taryn take the heat for his mistakes.

"What?" Talon said, turning to Toby.

"It wasn't her fault! So leave her the fuck alone!" Toby defended Taryn, standing up and getting in his brother's face.

"Boys, stop!" Terrance tried to calm his sons.

"No, this needs to come out," Toby said strongly. "I'm sorry I made you keep this a secret, Mom. I can't let you go through your final days with this weighing on you because of me," Toby said to Trisha, tears streaming down his face.

Talon and Terrance froze, and all eyes were on Toby.

"It was my fault our marriage ended," he repeated.

"But Taryn is the one that filed for divorce?" Terrance said, confused.

"Yes, but she filed for divorce so I could be happy," Toby began. Taking Annalee's hand in his, he continued. "Annalee and I were having an affair for a while before Taryn found out and continued to see each other even after I promised Taryn I wouldn't. Her sons became like my own, and three months after confessing everything to Taryn, I found out Annalee was pregnant with Ally. I told Taryn I would leave Annalee and fix things with her, but Ti knew that would make me more miserable than I already was with myself. I dug a hole so deep I had no way to get out. But Taryn... Taryn offered me that way out. She sacrificed her happiness, our marriage, and the relationships she built with a lot of people, mutual to both of us, so I could start a happy life with Annalee."

Toby's confession floored Talon and Terrance, and both of them collapsed back in their seats. Outspoken Talon was silent for the first time in his life as Terrance frowned, trying to comprehend his son's confession.

"Taryn, I'm so sorry. I shouldn't have let you take the heat for this for so long. I'm sorry for taking the easy way out and not manning up to my mistakes sooner," Toby said, turning his attention to Taryn with tears in his eyes.

"As long as you and Annalee are happy, it was worth it. Having this come out sooner, before the wedding, before the birth of Ally, would've been too stressful, and no life should start in such a mess. I'm okay. I promise. Just take care of each other, okay?" Taryn said, forcing a smile and trying to keep her own tears from erupting from her eyes as she looked between Toby and Annalee.

Taryn turned to Trisha, who was still clinging onto her hand, and smiled.

"Thank you for always seeing the best in me, even during doubtful times. You will always be the best mother-in-law I could've asked for, and I will cherish the memories I was lucky enough to share with you forever," Taryn said as a stray tear fell from her eye.

On a heavy sigh, Taryn released Trisha's hand and turned to leave. Without looking back or saying another word, she walked out of the door with her head held high. As she found herself entering the waiting room again, the expressions on everyone's face had shifted from anger to compassion and guilt as they landed on Taryn. Just as Talon and Terrance, the rest of the family was floored in utter shock and disbelief. They, too, had heard Toby's confession and didn't know how to approach Taryn anymore. Even his aunts and uncles sat there, completely stunned, unable to say anything to her.

"Ti, we're so sorry," Toby's cousin Carrie said for the group as she got up from her chair, crossed the waiting area, and hugged Taryn hard.

"It's fine," Taryn said, pulling away gently. "You were protecting your own. I get it. Don't worry about it."

Unable to say anything else, Taryn walked around Carrie and headed for the elevator. She could feel the family's eyes still on her back.

Just a little while longer. Hold it together, Ti, she thought as she waited for the elevator. She climbed in and finally exhaled, not even realizing she was holding her breath that entire time. Her knees grew weak as the elevator light signaled she was back at the lobby floor. Exiting the elevator, she rushed to her car across the parking lot, wanting to lock herself in and away from the world.

As she got into her car and shut the door, she collapsed onto the steering wheel sobbing. Tears and pain from the past year flowed from her uncontrollably, and everything crashed down on her at once as the horrible memories flooded her. Gasping for air already, she was unsure how she would ever stop. Her heart ached in her chest as the pain she kept bottled up for so long flowed through her veins, and she tried to regain control of herself.

Knock, knock, knock.

Petite knuckles rapped on her driver side window. Looking up, she saw her older cousin Jasmine, Jazzy for short, standing there with an empathetic look on her face. Jazzy backed up from the door as Taryn sprung from her car and into Jazzy's arms, her crying fit starting all over again.

"It's okay, Ti. Just breathe," Jazzy soothed.

Jazzy was Taryn's older cousin, godsister, and one of her ride-or-die best friends. There was so much that Jazzy stood by for her since she was born, that Taryn honestly would not know where she would be without her. After confessing the truth about the divorce to Nathan and coming home this week, Taryn spent an hour on the phone last night with Jazzy, telling her the truth about everything.

"How did you know I was here?" Taryn asked through her sobs.

"Nathan called me after he got the letter you left him, and he gave me the heads-up that you flew home early. I only realized this morning that you were already home when I was talking with you!" Jazzy fussed. "Then Lewie called and told me he heard you were coming here today. So I've been sitting in the parking lot, in my hot ass car this entire time, waiting for you to see if you needed me. When I saw you run out the way you did, big sis had to intervene," Jazzy said as she rubbed Taryn's back. "It didn't go so well, I'm guessing?"

"No, it did. But just everything…uh! It was too much. Trisha didn't look good, the whole family looked at me like they wanted me dead, and most of all, I felt like dirt seeing Toby with Annalee," Taryn admitted.

Jazzy just listened, nodding, letting Taryn get it all off her chest.

"What hurt the most was the fact that seeing them together confirmed that I did the right thing by divorcing Toby." Taryn scoffed. "A selfish part of me was hoping there would be utter turmoil and karma would ruin them, but by me removing myself from the picture, they were happy."

"Don't say that, Ti," Jazzy said. "Yes, they might be happy, but don't feel guilty for wanting them to suffer a little after everything they put you through."

"Well, they're suffering now." Taryn scoffed. "I just didn't want them to suffer this way. Trisha was too nice of a lady to go through this."

"If it makes you feel better, I have a surprise for you." Jazzy gave her a gentle smile.

"Unless you got a bottle of wine in your trunk and can find me a D2 driver right now, I'm not in the mood for any surprises," Taryn said as she slumped her back against her car door.

"You'll like this one, I promise," Jazzy said with a smile before nodding in the direction of Taryn's passenger side of the car.

She turned around, and tears began welling in Taryn's eyes again. Standing there with a duffle bag over his shoulder was Lewis. Without thinking, Taryn ran around the car and threw herself into his arms on a sob.

"What are you doing here?" she choked out.

"Well, after hanging up with Tyson, I called Kam's mom, Elaine, and told her I had a family emergency back home and arranged for her to take Kam a day early. I booked the red-eye last night and, yeah… Jazzy picked me up from the airport when I landed and we came straight here," Lewis said, squeezing comfort back into Taryn as she clung to his waist.

"Yep. He called me last night after I spoke to Nathan and told me he needed to come home to make sure you were okay. That's how I knew shit was serious," Jazzy said.

"Thank you," Taryn mumbled to Jazzy with Lewis's bicep pressed against her face.

"What was that, bitch? You're sorry I wasn't the first person you called when your ass decided to have a mental breakdown and fly home without telling anyone?" Jazzy said sarcastically. "It's okay, I forgive you, and you're welcome," she added as she walked around the car and began adding to the hug.

"I love you guys," Taryn sobbed.

"All right, enough crying. Your eyes are going to get puffy, and you're inhaling all the airplane germs that are still on my shirt," Lewis said, breaking up the group hug. "Let's get you home," he added, taking Taryn's keys from her hand.

"Call me when you guys get there, okay?" Jazzy called out to Lewis as she headed for her own car.

"Will do," Lewis replied.

Taryn climbed into her passenger seat as Lewis threw his duffle in the back. Climbing into the driver seat, he sat there for a moment, taking Taryn's hand in his and giving it a little squeeze of support.

"I know you're not okay, so I'm not going to ask. Just know I got you," Lewis said to her as he lifted her hand and kissed her knuckles gently.

"Thanks," Taryn said gratefully as she settled back into the seat.

Lewis started the car and pulled out of the parking lot, getting Taryn far away from the mess left at the hospital.

4

Lewis

Lewis drove down the highway to take Taryn home. The sun began to set, shining a warm ray of light through her windshield that made her glow with a different type of beauty as she took a nap in the passenger seat. The ocean looked breathtaking, nothing like the ocean you see back in California. Rolling the window down, he inhaled the salty air as the sounds of the waves crashing in the distance calmed him. Running into Taryn at K-Elements was the first time Lewis had seen or spoken to her in almost ten years. Aside from seeing her occasional posts on social media, he pulled back from their friendship dramatically after she had met Toby. It just hurt too much to try and be her friend when she was still with him, and after becoming a father, his priorities changed. Kam became the center of his being and gave his life meaning for the first time.

Lewis was four years older than Taryn, and his next-door neighbor was her uncle, Taryn's mom's oldest brother. Throughout elementary and middle school, Lewis would see her occasionally when they came over to her uncle's for family parties, but he didn't really notice her until her senior year of high school. It was as if overnight, she had blossomed from this nerdy kid into a full-grown woman, but the one thing that never changed was the amount of kindness she had in her heart. Despite her tough exterior, the extent of her kindness could always be seen in the depth of her eyes. Even if everyone in Hawai'i was brought up to care for each other as one big family, Taryn took it to another level. Whether it was helping a neighbor, staying after school to volunteer, or driving a distance to be a shoulder to lean on, she could always be counted on for her loyalty and ability to follow through for those she cared about when they needed her the most. It was a level of kindness that was reserved for those closest to her and Lewis was lucky to experience it first-hand.

That year before she met her ex-husband, Lewis remembered being really sick right before his birthday. It was college midterms for Taryn, and she was balancing studying with working two jobs to put herself through school. When she found out that Lewis was sick, she drove forty-five minutes to his house to bring him dinner and take care of him. He never had a girl do that for him before. What shocked him the most was Taryn thought nothing of it; she was just taking care of someone she cared about. She was truly one of a kind, always finding a way to be there for the people around her, regardless of what was going on in her own life.

Glancing over at Taryn, he smiled despite himself. Even without trying, at peace asleep, she could make his heart skip a beat. If there was one regret he had in his life, it was not telling her how he actually felt all those years ago. Although he'd never admit it out loud to anyone or even officially confirm it to his friends or to himself, he knew deep in his heart that he had fallen for her, that there was always more than mere friendship between them. He just never told her how he felt. Everyone kept saying that she felt the same, that they'd make a good couple since they had so much history and had a strong friendship already, but he couldn't ever bring himself to do it. She was too special to him, and he never wanted to cross that line, never wanted to risk messing it up and losing her friendship altogether. He'd rather have her friendship than not have her in his life at all, but once Toby came into the picture, he lost her anyways. He shook his head with regret, as he turned down the street to her house.

Lewis pulled into her driveway. He opened the garage door with the remote in her center console. He hadn't been here for years. Aside from the recent paint job, the house still looked the same.

"Ti, we're home," Lewis said as he gently shook her arm.

"Sorry. I didn't even realize I fell asleep," she said, rubbing the sleep from her eyes. "Wow, you remembered where I lived?"

"Of course," he said with a smile. "Coming here every weekend in high school to help with your grandma's yard work or go fishing on the boat, how could I ever forget?"

Taryn lived with her parents at her grandmother Patricia's house her entire life, aside from when she moved in with Toby when they were married. When Taryn was five, Tiana and Noah were looking to purchase their own house. Tiana was pregnant with Nathan at the time, so they needed more space. But when Tiana's father died suddenly, she couldn't leave Patricia when she needed her the most. So they stayed, building an extension to the house on the large family property to give their growing family more room. A year ago, when Taryn moved back home after separating from Toby, they built a second master suite downstairs, toward the back end of the house with a walk-in closet, full bathroom, and her own small living-office area. It wasn't much and wasn't the freedom and independence she had strived for her whole life, but it was home, and she was grateful to have it.

As they entered the foyer, Lewis gasped at what he saw. It wasn't the old-school home with brown shag carpet and creaky wooden cabinets throughout that he remembered. The inside was completely renovated with new white quartz countertops, light-gray cabinets, and dark wooden floors. Even the furniture all looked new. The space was completely transformed.

"Whoa! When did you guys do this?" Lewis exclaimed.

"Over the last year. Since I needed a place to stay after separating from Toby, Mom guys closed off the extended back patio to make a room for me," Taryn started, pointing past the living space and stairs down a small hallway. "So to say thank you, I used some of the money from the divorce to renovate the house for them. Friends, neighbors, and my uncles, of course, all pitched in to do the labor work. It was a fun project to get done, a good stress relief too."

"Wait, you guys did this yourselves?" Lewis asked, surprised.

"Yes," Taryn said sarcastically. "Sometimes when I couldn't sleep at night, I'd be up tiling or painting things. It just occupied my mind in the right ways, you know?"

"Damn, Ti. I don't talk to you for ten years and suddenly you're a handywoman, doctor, and teacher?" Lewis laughed.

Taryn playfully pushed Lewis and laughed despite herself as she slid onto one of the barstools by the kitchen island.

"Okay, what do you want for dinner? You look like hell right now, and I know for a fact that 99 percent chance is you haven't eaten yet. So what'll it be?" Lewis asked.

"It's okay, Lewis. I'm not hungry," Taryn replied.

"When's the last time you ate?" he retorted.

"I had a cranberry vodka on the plane with a bag of pretzels," she said innocently. "Does that count?"

"No, that doesn't count!" Lewis exclaimed. "But I don't feel right just digging in your fridge anymore, so how about I order us some pizza?"

"That never bothered you before." Taryn laughed. "I remember you used to come over sometimes and just walk right up to the fridge to grab leftovers to eat."

"Ti, that was ages ago." He scoffed. "I have manners now."

"Sure you do." She teased.

"Hey, you can't blame me though. Your grandma is an amazing cook! I would've been so fat if I had lived here." He laughed as he leaned his elbows on the counter.

"True! If it weren't for me doing club cheer and having those four-hour practices five times a week from middle school, I would've been an Oompa-Loompa!" Taryn laughed.

"Shit, I forgot about that. I remember having to drive Jazzy to pick your ass up from practice sometimes when your parents would be waiting for you and eating dinner at your uncle's house," Lewis thought back, reminiscing. "For a girl, you would be so stink sometimes when we'd come and get you! Especially around your competition season when you guys would do your routine over and over again. I think your sweat smells might still be clinging to the fabric in my old car," he teased.

"Wow," Taryn said sarcastically before laughing. "I did reek sometimes, huh?"

"Yes, you did, but your passion and dedication to the sport was commendable," Lewis acknowledged.

"I miss it." Taryn sighed.

"Cheer?" Lewis questioned.

"Yes." She nodded. "To lose yourself in the music, to tumble and stunt, feeling like you're flying when you defy gravity. It was all so freeing."

"Do you still keep in touch with your coaches and teammates?" Lewis asked.

"We text all the time. I've even gone to a few of their practices to get a workout in after the divorce," she replied with a smile. "They'll always be a second family to me."

"Okay, well, why don't you go get cleaned up? Go shower and I'll call the pizza in. Pepperoni mushroom with extra cheese, right?" Lewis said.

"You remember?" Taryn asked, glancing over her shoulder with a smile.

"I'd never forget," Lewis replied with a wink.

5

Taryn

After a long hot shower and throwing some shorts and a tank top on, Taryn emerged from her room. Lewis had turned on the air conditioner in the house, and the coolness felt nice on her skin. She walked toward the kitchen island as she continued to dry her hair with a towel. Lewis emerged from the front door with a box of pizza and a container of hot wings in his hand.

"Mmm! Wings!" Taryn said excitedly as she wiggle-danced in her seat.

"Right? You can't have pizza without the wings," Lewis said, setting the food down in front of her.

"Did you get—" Taryn started.

"Ranch?" Lewis finished for her.

"You always did know me so well, huh?" She smiled as she gave her hair a few last squeezes with her towel.

"Only weirdos would eat pizza and wings without ranch," he teased.

The old friends burst out into laughter. Among their group of friends, they were the only ones who shared a love for ranch dressing. Whether it be on salad, wings, or tacos, they always had to order a side of ranch with almost every meal. Even after ten years, nothing seemed to have changed. They picked up right where they left off.

"You ready to eat then?" Lewis said, walking behind Taryn and taking the towel and draping it over the chair next to her.

27

"I guess," Taryn said with a heavy sigh, leaning back into Lewis's chest. She could feel his muscles tense beneath her head.

"Ti, you gotta eat. Even if that means I have to force-feed the pizza down your throat," Lewis said, taking her head between his hands and tilting her head backward so he could look into her eyes.

Taryn just smiled and sighed as she stared into the familiar brown eyes that could always comfort her.

"Come on," Lewis said, kissing her on the forehead. "I'm going to watch you eat, and then I'll call an Uber to take me to my dad's place."

"What? Why?" Taryn asked. She sat up and turned to him, confused.

"Because that's where I stay when I come home. Besides, I'm only here until Sunday, so I figure I could spend tomorrow with my dad," Lewis replied.

"Lewis, you can just sleep over here. I can drive you home in the morning," Taryn stated. "It's almost eight o'clock already, and an Uber from here to your dad's place is going to be ridiculous. If you really gotta go home tonight, I can drive you after we eat."

"Nope, not happening. You know I don't like you driving at night," Lewis retorted.

"Okay, so just stay here. It's not a big deal," Taryn argued.

Suddenly, she got up and headed to her room before Lewis could retort. After a few minutes, she emerged with pieces of clothing in her hands.

"See? I still have your basketball shorts and hoodie. I'll grab you a clean towel. You can shower in my bathroom and you'll be good. And you know I always have a spare toothbrush," Taryn said, coming back to the kitchen holding Lewis's old clothes.

Whenever Taryn would sleep over in the past, it was always unplanned. Either she was too drunk to drive home, or it would get too late for her to drive after binge-watching Netflix or movies. So she would always borrow clothes from him to sleep in and rarely returned them. But even after she got married, Taryn could never find it in herself to get rid of his clothes or give them back. She would still even use his hoodies from time to time.

"You still have my clothes?" Lewis laughed, taking them.

"Of course," Taryn said with a soft smile.

"I don't know though, Ti. I feel like I should still go home tonight," Lewis said, unsure of himself.

"Lewis...please," Taryn said, suddenly sad. "If I'm being honest, I just don't want to be alone tonight. Not after today. I just need a friend."

Taryn's eyes started to glaze over as the tightness in his heart began to show on Lewis's face. She knew he couldn't tell her no. He flew all the way from California to make sure she was okay; there was no way he would leave if she was still upset.

"Fine." He finally sighed. "But tomorrow you come hang out with me and the family, okay? It's been a while, and I know they miss you. Plus, I think it's the annual summer barbeque tomorrow too if I remember correctly so it's perfect."

"Deal," Taryn said with a grateful smile.

"Come here," Lewis replied, walking over to Taryn at the edge of the living room couch and embracing her. "It'll be okay. I promise."

"I hope so," Taryn said.

*****

The pizza and wings were perfect. Taryn cracked open a bottle of white wine for them to drink as they ate. Their conversation was a blur of "remember when" stories mixed with ten years' worth of updates on life.

Lewis shared that he split from Elaine, his daughter's mom, after Kam's second birthday. It was her idea to move up to California five years ago when she was pregnant with Kam, to have "more opportunities," but upon moving, she began to change. He didn't go into details about what happened but noted that it just didn't work out. Lewis was heartbroken. He was going to propose to her and had already gotten Elaine a ring when they called it quits. Three years later, they finally learned to coparent effectively as friends.

Taryn spilled all her secrets about her divorce, going into even more detail about how she found out about Toby's affair, her thoughts on Annalee's pregnancy, and how, when it all happened, she some-times felt so depressed, she felt as if she wanted to kill herself. So she would force smiles more so the people around her wouldn't know. She also confessed to him how hard it had been taking the wrap for everything, biting her tongue each time fingers were pointed at her but how it was what was best.

"Wow." Lewis sighed after hearing it all. "You really are some-thing else. I've never known you to bite your tongue."

"Right? Not for anyone," Taryn admitted, shocked at herself. "I just keep kept thinking about the baby though. That no child should be brought into a world full of that much turmoil. It was just easier to be the bad guy."

"So you didn't do it for them? For Annalee and Toby?" Lewis asked.

"Nope, I don't think so." Taryn thought hard about her answer.

"Well, whatever your reason, Ti, you are a better person than I could ever be," Lewis replied. "When things didn't work out with Elaine, I wanted to rip someone's throat out. I had moved up there for her, away from my family and everyone for nothing, you know? I had to go to anger management courses so I didn't take my anger out on Kam, but that anger just ended up being channeled into being an overprotective dad. So I guess it all worked out."

"Kam is lucky to have you for a dad, Lewis," Taryn said sin-cerely. "Even if I can't picture you as a dad. I still see you as that tough, player, eye-candy version of you from ten years ago," she added jokingly.

"Hey! I wasn't a player," Lewis retorted.

"Yes, you were." Taryn scoffed. "If only you knew how many girls fell for your conflicting 'I'm sweet, but I'm a bad boy' act. You had girls drooling at your feet."

"Okay, so you're right about that. I did play that role, but I never acted on it. Like I never slept around, and when I was in rela-tionships, I was committed to that person," Lewis argued.

"What do you call what we did then, Lewis? That wasn't sleep-ing around with each other?" Taryn questioned.

"No." Lewis sighed uncomfortably, looking down.

"Then what would you call it? We weren't together. We were literally just fuck buddies," Taryn pushed.

"No, we weren't," Lewis said solemnly. "I could have deep conversations with you, talk about things that no one else would understand, study together, just cuddle watching movies and stuff. You weren't just a fuck buddy to me. I would never disrespect you or your family like that. And if you think that of me, I'm not sure how well you actually know me then, Ti."

Taryn was confused. She sat back, paused, and took a hard stare at Lewis. His face showed that her accusations had truly hurt him somehow. Was he trying to tell her that he saw her as more than just a friend? She knew that she had feelings for him, but because of his playboy reputation with their group of friends, she never expected more from him than what it was and just grew to enjoy his company in whatever form it came. Since she was single and he was good at it, she just thought the sex was just a fun sort-of bonus to their friendship. They grew up together, and she felt comfortable enough doing that with him, trusted him enough to know he'd stand by her if anything happened, and still have that friendship without things getting too weird.

"Lewis, what are you saying then?" Taryn wondered out loud after a long silence.

"Nothing. Just drop it, please," he replied, getting up and starting to clear the island.

Sitting there stunned, she watched him put away the leftovers, wash the wine glasses, and rinse out the wine bottle, all without so much as a glance in her direction. When he was done, he stood at the edge of the island, gripping the countertop as if he wanted to say something but just couldn't get it past his lips. He let out a heavy sigh.

"Lewis?" Taryn said gently, walking over and resting her hand on his, her fingers slowly tracing the tribal tattoo design on his wrist. "I'm sorry if I upset you."

"It's nothing, Ti. Don't worry," he replied with a shrug.

Pulling his hand away from hers, he walked over to the couch where she had placed his clothes and headed into her room to shower.

Unsure of what else to do, she stopped at the linen closet in the hall-way to grab him a towel before following him into her room. She stopped at the locked bathroom door before she sighed. It was as if the whole world was either hurt because of her or wanted to hurt her and she began to hate herself more for it. She couldn't bring pain into Lewis's life too. He was the one person she was sure she never wanted to hurt again.

6

Lewis

Sitting on her toilet, Lewis took deep breaths over and over again, trying to calm himself. Being with Taryn was so easy. They got along so well, and even after ten years, it was as if no time had passed. Yet hearing her think she was just a fuck buddy to him—or worse, the fact that she might have only seen him as a fuck buddy—hurt more than separating from Elaine and having to figure out how to co-parent. Lewis knew he still cared about Taryn and would check on her through social media often over the last ten years, but he had convinced himself that his old feelings for her were long gone, that they never existed. Tonight over dinner, he realized he was highly mistaken. There was a knock on the door, and Taryn's gentle voice pulled him from his thoughts.

"Lewis? I got you a towel," she said softly.

With a heavy sigh, he got up and walked over to the door. Listening to her breathing heavily on the other side, he looked to the ground to see the shadow from her feet fidgeting uncomfortably, seemingly anxious. He had to get himself together quickly before he faced her, even if it was just for a towel, or he would crumble at her feet. Lewis knew that would just make things worse for Taryn right now, and he didn't want to open that hypothetical door again if he didn't know she felt the same way.

"I love you, Taryn," he whispered to himself as he rested his head on the closed door. He knew she couldn't hear him, and he didn't want to say it to her face. Lewis just needed to get it off his chest so he wasn't tempted to blurt it out randomly to her.

Slowly, he opened the bathroom door. Taryn's big brown eyes filled her face with concern as her hair cascaded gently over her shoulders. Her hand held out a fluffy gray towel as a peace offering.

"Thank you," Lewis said to her as he leaned down and kissed her on the cheek. "I'll be out in a few."

*****

Despite the Hawai'i humidity, Lewis threw the shower on full blast, letting the hot water nearly burn his skin. He wanted to feel numb. Deep inside, he knew he only came home to support Taryn because his feelings for her were still strong, but he would never be able to admit that to her out loud. After allowing the hot water to calm him, Lewis showered quickly. The soap cascaded down his face and body, cleansing his countless tattoos but not washing away the scars and pain he felt in his heart. Jumping out of the shower and drying off, he threw on his old clothes that Taryn had saved. To his surprise, despite the clothes being a little tight around the military muscles he'd developed over the years, they fit more or less. Finding her hamper, he lifted the lid to throw his dirty towel in when a red lacy thong caught his attention. He could feel the blood rush down to his crotch, and his cock immediately budged forward in his shorts.

"Great," Lewis said to himself sarcastically. "Fucking free balling it is going to be the death of me tonight." He huffed.

Lewis adjusted and pushed himself down in his shorts and exited the bathroom, expecting to find Taryn asleep in her bed. But her room was empty. He made his way to the living room and kitchen; she was nowhere to be found. Concerned, he began calling out her name.

"Ti? Ti? Are you here?" Lewis said.

He went out to the garage, checked the backyard, and even went upstairs and checked the other rooms. Yet he could still not find her. *How long was I in that damn shower?* Lewis thought. Coming into the kitchen, he found Taryn's phone plugged into the wall charger, her screen flashing over and over again with countless messages and missed calls.

"Nope. Don't do it, Lewie-boy. It's not your business," he said to himself, trying to talk himself down from the temptation of going through her phone.

Instead, he simply stared at the phone. Toby's name popped up multiple times, as did Jazzy's, her brother Nathan's, and someone named Derek. Unable to control his urge any longer, he reached for her phone and attempted to unlock it.

"Come on, Lewis. You know Ti. What would her password be?" he thought out loud, staring at the phone.

He needed a four-number code to get in. Suddenly, he remembered that Taryn used different seasons and episodes from her favorite show *Criminal Minds*. So, if it was season 1 episode 1, her code would be 0101. Thinking hard, he remembered her favorite episode of all time. It was the hundredth episode of the series, where the main character, Hotch, had to face off with a notorious serial killer to save his family. It was the ninth episode of the fifth season.

"Please work," Lewis said as he typed in 0509.

It worked! He opened her text messages and immediately found the ones from Toby. After what Toby and his family put Taryn through today, Lewis expected him to leave her alone for good. She finally got closure today with Toby's family finding out the truth, so what more could this jerk want from Taryn?

"Taryn, thank you for coming by today. It was really good to see you." (Toby)

"I'm sorry that me being there caused drama with your family. Are you and Annalee okay?" (Taryn)

"We're okay. It's just going to be a transition for us moving forward. Annalee has to redeem herself in the eyes of my family, but since we have a baby together, they're kind of forced to accept her now whether or not they like her." (Toby)

"True, but don't be like your brother and use your kid as leverage to force your family to accept you guys. Give them time." (Taryn)

"Thanks Ti for being so understanding and for the advice. You're the perfect godmother for my daughter." (Toby)

"Wait, what?" (Taryn)

"Annalee and I want you to be the godmother in case anything ever happens to us. It was originally my mom, but she passed shortly after you left the hospital. It was like she was waiting to say sorry to you before she could leave this earth peacefully." (Toby)

"HOLD ON! So you're telling me, in ONE TEXT that 1, I'm the godmother for your kid (without even asking me) and 2, your mom passed after I left? WHAT THE HELL IS WRONG WITH YOU? You don't tell someone that via text let alone loop those two things in together!" (Taryn)

"Well, the two things are related, and I didn't think you'd want me calling you. This way too, you can't really say no." (Toby)

"Goodbye Toby." (Taryn)

"Ti?" (Toby)

"Taryn?" (Toby)

"Hello?" (Toby)

"What the fuck?" Lewis said out loud. He couldn't believe the nerve of Toby. "No wonder she left her fucking phone here! Damnit!"

Going into full panic mode, Lewis yanked Taryn's phone from the charger, grabbed his phone and her keys, and rushed to the garage. Barely waiting for the garage door to open, he reversed quickly into the street, the dark night sky casting a heavy shadow over the road.

Once he saw the garage door begin to lower, he sped down the road to the traffic light.

He dialed Jazzy frantically over and over again, trying to get some clue as to where Taryn could have gone. It couldn't have been that far since she didn't take her car. But when she was upset, she could walk and wander for miles at a time and disappear without a trace quickly. He remembered one New Year's Eve, she had gotten drunk and upset at her brother and ended up walking almost three miles to sit on the swings at a park just so she could look at the stars.

The stars! That was always her go-to when she needed to clear her mind! The memory hit him like a train. But there were so many places on the westside where she lived that had beautiful views of the stars. He didn't know where to start and didn't have time to guess. Taking her phone and punching the code in again, he called her brother.

"Hello? Ti? You okay? Isn't it like eleven over there?" Nathan's voice came over the speaker.

"Hey, Nathan. It's Lewis Rivera. Taryn and Jazzy's friend? The one that lived next to your uncle?" Lewis explained hastily, hearing voices in the background on the call.

"Lewis? Yeah, I remember you. What are you doing with Taryn's phone? She hasn't even called me, and yet you are?" Nathan sounded confused as Lewis heard him try and hush whoever he was with so he could hear better.

"It's a long story, but I'm back in Hawai'i, and Taryn just went missing. She went to pay respects to Toby's mom earlier this afternoon in the hospital. Apparently, Toby's dumb ass started to text her about an hour ago, telling her that his mom passed after she left and because his mom passed, she was now the godmother to his daughter!" Lewis summed up with frustration.

"What the fuck?" Nathan yelled.

"Is she okay?" another male's voice was frantic and could be heard in the distance.

"I don't think so. I came out of the shower and she disappeared. She goes and looks at the stars when she needs to clear her mind when life is too much to handle, but I don't know where she would go right now! There're too many beaches out your guys' side for me to search." Lewis was almost frantic.

"You showered at our house?" Nathan questioned.

"Yes, I drove her home after the hospital," Lewis said, exasperated. "Now which beach, Nathan? Focus, please!"

"Go to the traffic light at the end of our street. Cross over the highway into the beach parking lot. Walk across the grass to the tree that is in line with the traffic light. From there, walk about ten feet out onto the sand toward the water, then turn left and walk about fifty yards down until you are behind the house with the tiki torch lights lining their property. At the far right corner of their lot, where their stone wall meets the sand, in the shadows, there's a huge smooth boulder. You'll find Taryn there," Nathan replied.

"Thank you." Lewis sighed as he pulled into a stall at the beach park across the street from Taryn's house.

"Lewis, can you keep me on the phone until you find her?" Nathan asked as Lewis parked and got out of the car, following the directions given to him.

"Sure, give me a few," Lewis replied as he walked into the darkness toward the beach. "You sure she'll be there?"

"I'm sure. That's her secret spot. No one knows about it except me, and now you, I guess. I followed her out there one night after she got into a huge fight with Mom, and every time she'd disappear when stuff was going on, I could find her there," Nathan explained.

"Okay, I'm almost there. I see the torches," Lewis stated as Nathan listened patiently on the other end of the line.

"Okay," Nathan said, waiting.

As Lewis got closer, he saw the big boulder off to the right of the last torch in the shadows. Taryn was sitting there, hugging her knees with her head leaning back against the wall and staring at the sky. Tears were clearly streaming down her face, her sobs muffled by the sound of the waves crashing on the reef.

"I got her," Lewis told Nathan as he got closer.

"Can I talk to her real quick?" Nathan said.

"Sure. Give me a second," Lewis replied.

He came to a stop in front of the boulder. Taryn turned her puffy eyes to Lewis. They were full of pain, glistening wet from her tears in the moonlight, that made Lewis's heart ache. Her cheeks were red, her hair a distraught mess around her face from crying.

"Hey," she sighed, taking deep breaths and trying to stop herself from crying. "I guess you found me, huh?"

"Nathan's on the phone," Lewis said, handing her cell phone to her.

Lewis couldn't make out what Nathan was telling her, but Taryn nodded and said her I'm sorrys, okays, and I promises before hanging up the phone and shoving it into the pocket of her hoodie.

"Can I sit?" Lewis asked gently.

"Sure." Taryn nodded as she scooted over to give Lewis some space to squeeze in next to her.

"I saw the texts from Toby," Lewis confessed as he pulled his knees up to his chest.

"I figured," Taryn replied. "Nathan told me. I'm not surprised you cracked my password." She scoffed.

"I told you. I still know you. Just because time has passed, it doesn't mean I suddenly forgot about you." Lewis sighed heavily. "Taryn, you were such a huge part of my life, and you still are. Our friendship just had a prolonged speed bump that we had to get over, and now it's all good."

"Lewis," Taryn said softly, turning to him and squeezing his arm. Her voice was breaking.

"You don't gotta say anything, Ti." Lewis smiled.

"How did I survive the last ten years without you?" Taryn replied, tears starting to fill her eyes.

"Come here," Lewis said, spreading his knees apart and pulling her between them.

Taryn nestled between his legs. Lewis pulled her to lean backward, her head resting on his chest. He wrapped his arms around her, squeezing comfort back into her on a heavy sigh as she held onto his forearms spread across her chest for support. Lewis could feel her body shake as they sat together, a thousand thoughts being shared in utter silence.

"You getting cold?" Lewis asked. Despite it being Hawai'i, nights on the open beach with the ocean breezes could get pretty chilly.

Taryn nodded yes against his chest.

"Let's get you home then," Lewis said, pulling out his phone to check the time. "It's after midnight already."

She followed his lead and reluctantly got up from the safety and comfort of his embrace. Lewis stood up and stretched, his hoodie lifting and flashing his carved abs at her and the tattoo of a koi fish surfing that he had stupidly gotten on a dare back in high school on the dip of his hip. He could see Taryn smile. The moonlight kissed her skin and made her glow as if she were an angel. He offered his hand to her after getting blood back into his legs, and she took it gratefully. Leading the way, Lewis walked her to the parking lot. With one hand in his, Taryn wrapped her other hand around his bicep and hugged his arm to her until they got to the car.

"I can't believe you called Nathan," Taryn said, laughing to herself as she got into the passenger seat. Lewis started the car. "Are you trying to get me in trouble?"

"I didn't know who else to call. Jazzy's ass wasn't answering her phone," Lewis said sarcastically.

"Well, thank you for doing that, for finding me," Taryn said with a half smile, the sadness still clear in her eyes.

"Anytime," Lewis said as he drove back across the street and pulled into her garage.

"Lew?" Taryn said before they got out of the car.

"Yes?" He hesitated with his hand on the door handle.

"I'm really glad you're here with me tonight," she said as she sighed and stepped out of the car.

The two of them headed into the house, going straight to the guest bathroom right off the garage door. They jumped in together. Lewis turned on the faucet and squeezed some soap onto their feet. He knew her too well and knew she would not walk into the house, let alone let him come in, without washing the sand off first. Lewis smiled to himself, thinking of the two of them just falling back into such a simple habit without thinking. After wiping their feet, Taryn pulled extra pillows and a blanket out of the linen closet and placed it on the couch for him.

"Good night," Lewis said to her as she turned to walk away.

"Good night." She smiled over her shoulder before disappearing into her room.

7

Derek

It had been more than forty-eight hours since he had heard from Taryn, the last being the letter she wrote to him that basically tore his heart out of his body and crushed it. He tried to feel close to her and get any updates he could on what was going on, so he had been hanging out more and more with Nathan, Sienna, and Luke at night when he was done filming. Since their parents headed off to bed early, it left Nathan free to still go out at night.

Tonight, they were at a small tiki bar down the road from Nathan and Taryn's apartment. It was the perfect distraction for Derek. He was out, but it wasn't so crowded where he would feel overwhelmed. About an hour before the bar was to close, Nathan got a strange call. Taryn's name popped up on his screen. Seeing this, the four of them put cash down to cover the remainder of their tab and walked outside. Sienna and Luke were arguing among themselves about who could handle more alcohol, even if they were both wasted. Derek clung to Nathan's side, trying to hear Taryn's voice. Instead, the panicked voice of a man came across the line, making Derek's heart race.

"It's Lewis," the man's voice hastened. Derek couldn't hear much else.

"Lewis?" Nathan's response confirmed it.

Derek's heart dropped full force to the sidewalk as the blood drained from his body. Everything started to move in slow motion. Taryn was hurt seeing him kiss Lexie on Wednesday, so now she went running back to her friend Lewis? Ananya said she overheard that Lewis had feelings for Taryn, but Ti made it very clear that they were just friends. So why was she running back to him? Did she not go home? Did she just go to stay with Lewis for a while? A thousand questions started going through Derek's head, and he started to feel nauseous.

"What the fuck?" Nathan's response to Lewis snapped Derek out of his trance.

"Is she okay?" Derek's eyes pleaded for Nathan to tell him something, anything. His own insecurities shot out the window with the thought that something terrible had happened to Taryn.

"Taryn's missing," Nathan whispered as he covered the microphone with his hand.

Derek's world started spinning as he began to stumble backward. As his back collided with the concrete wall, his knees began to give out as he slumped down onto the sidewalk. Sienna and Luke, no longer oblivious to what was transpiring, each bolted to be beside Derek and Nathan.

"She's missing," Derek said softly to himself. Luke and Sienna's eyes went wide with worry of their own now.

"Lewis, can you keep me on the phone until you find her?" Nathan's voice broke through their panic as they all stared, frozen in the moment and waiting for an update.

After what seemed like forever, Nathan nodded.

"He found her," he whispered, covering the mic again. "Can I talk to her real quick?" Nathan asked Lewis.

There was another long pause. Nathan put the phone on speaker so everyone could hear, putting one finger to his mouth to silently tell everyone to stay quiet as he spoke to his sister.

"Ti, you okay? What the fuck happened? Why haven't you called me yet since you got home? Are you okay?" Nathan questioned, his voice soaked in concern.

"I'm okay," Taryn replied softly. You could tell that she had been crying. Her breath was faltering.

"Let Lewis take you home already. The beach isn't safe by yourself, dumbass!" Nathan barked down the phone.

"Okay." Taryn sighed, agreeing without contesting.

"You're going to call me tomorrow, like you promised you'd do when you landed, and you're going to tell me everything. Including what the fuck Toby told you that set you off," Nathan continued.

"Okay." Taryn sighed heavily.

"Stop just saying okay! Promise you'll call. Don't just disappear again," Nathan scolded his older sister.

"I promise," Taryn replied.

"Okay. Home now and call tomorrow. Got it?" Nathan fussed.

"Okay, I promise," Taryn said before hanging up the phone.

Clenching his phone, Nathan clenched his eyes shut and took some deep breaths to calm himself down. Since her divorce, she was suddenly like the younger sibling. She was irrational, impulsive, and did things that sent his blood pressure through the roof with worry. Nathan didn't know how to deal with her sometimes, and his anger often got the best of him.

"She's okay," Sienna soothed. "That's the main thing."

"Who's Lewis?" Luke hiccupped.

"He's an old family friend. Him, Ti, all my older cousins around their age were super close growing up. They were pretty much inseparable before she met Toby," Nathan replied cautiously, looking in Derek's direction.

"And he's in Hawai'i? At your house?" Luke slurred.

"Yeah. He flew home when he heard what was going down with Toby. I'm assuming Taryn told our cousin Jazzy when she landed and Jazzy ratted? I'm not sure how he knew. But I'm glad his ass was in Hawai'i. If not, who knows what would happen if Taryn stayed at that beach by herself any longer," Nathan thought out loud.

"Well, I'm glad he was there for her," Sienna said, glaring at Derek. Nathan told her about Derek's kiss with his ex, and he automatically lost brownie points with Sienna. Though she never made things awkward when the parents were around, she gave Derek evil eyes whenever she got a chance, defending Taryn endlessly.

*****

44

The four of them took an Uber back to Derek's apartment so they could continue to hang out without worrying about waking Nathan's parents. Luke passed out in front of the fireplace shortly after they got there, and Sienna helped herself to a bowl of instant spicy ramen in his kitchen. Nathan and Derek sat at the dining room table. Derek was unable to hide the troublesome thoughts that were bothering him.

"Lewis is just a friend." Nathan surprisingly tried to comfort Derek. "One thing you gotta understand is that in Hawai'i, your closest friends are like your family, and when family is in trouble, you drop everything to be there for them. That's how close Lewis and Taryn were."

"It's just hard for me to understand. Them being that close and not catching feelings for one another? I mean, I spent twenty-four hours with your sister and I couldn't help but start to fall in love with her," Derek tried to explain his thoughts.

"Did you just say you're in love with my sister?" Nathan questioned, sitting up in his chair.

He paused and thought back to what just came out of his mouth, and he realized that he did say that. Derek also realized in that moment that that's what he felt for Taryn. He was falling in love with her.

"Yes, I did." Derek sighed, surprised with his own openness.

"Wow," Nathan said, sitting back in utter shock. "Well, if you love her, I guess I better clue you in on the last forty-eight hours. You're going to have to know what a mess her life has turned into if you're going to help her pick up the pieces so she can fall in love with you too."

"I would really appreciate that, but why are you helping me? I thought you said you wanted me to stay away from her?" Derek questioned, confused.

"I actually got to spend some quality time with you so I could see for myself if you're a really good guy instead of just taking your sister's word for it. I'd be cool with you ending up with my sister. It seems like you really do care about her. You worry about her, you took care of her when she needed it the most, you supported her, and you haven't passed judgment on her once with everything that's been dumped on you since you met her," Nathan said.

"Thanks, Nate. That means a lot to me, more than I can explain," Derek replied.

"Eh, don't worry about it. Just don't break her heart. Put it back together if anything, okay?" Nathan replied.

"Aw! Look at you two. Bonding like lovers. I'm still mad at you though, D!" Sienna's drunken voice shattered their brotherly moment as she plopped down with her spicy ramen bowl. "Don't worry. I turned off the stove! Promise!"

As Sienna sat there satisfying her drunchies, Nathan told Derek everything. He explained to Derek as much as he got out of Jazzy when he called to see if Taryn had checked in with her. He told Derek about the phone call that she got after she left his set, why Taryn rushed home, what happened at the hospital, and about the texts Toby sent to Taryn that Lewis found on her phone this evening. Her hell had started with seeing Derek and Lexie kiss, but Taryn's past came back full force to try and drown her. Derek was no longer jealous of Lewis being with Taryn back in Hawai'i. He was more appreciative of Lewis than anything right now. Derek hated himself for being selfish and feeling hurt that she didn't let him explain. No wonder why she wasn't returning his texts or calls. Taryn was going through it, and Derek was surprised that she hadn't broken sooner. He knew he wouldn't be able to handle all that. Who knew so much damage could be done in a mere forty-eight hours?

8

Lewis

Lewis was mentally and emotionally exhausted. He knew he made the right choice coming home to support Taryn, but he didn't realize how much of an emotional roller coaster it would be for himself. He forced himself into the friend zone, and it was taking everything he had to make sure he didn't cross the line. Taryn needed a friend right now, nothing more, and he wanted to be that comfort for her.

He had been tossing and turning on the couch since they'd said their good nights. Lewis stared at the clock on the cable box. It was a quarter past 2:00 a.m. already. Sighing heavily, Lewis yanked off the hoodie, hoping the cool night air would calm him as he clenched his eyes shut, yearning for sleep to take him. In the silence of the night, Lewis suddenly heard faint noises coming from the hallway leading to Taryn's room. He got up quietly to investigate.

As he got closer, his heart sank. Taryn's sobs were clearer the closer he got to her door. *Should I knock?* he thought as he stood in front of the piece of wood, the only thing keeping him from making sure she was okay. Without thinking twice about it, he knocked gently on the door, and he turned the knob to let himself in.

"Ti?" Lewis whispered just in case she was asleep. "Are you okay?"

He walked closer to her bed, and his sunken heart crumbled completely, bringing him to his knees next to where she lay. Taryn was crying in her sleep, the emotions she pushed down in her subconscious pouring out without her waking mind to control them. Seeing her cry this way was like watching a newborn puppy being drowned. Lewis just wanted to wrap her in his arms and take away all the pain she was feeling.

"Taryn," he said gently as he leaned forward so his face was just inches from hers. He rubbed her arm softly to wake her.

Startled and unsure of where she was, Taryn shot up from her bed, getting tangled in the mess of blankets around her. Freaking out even more, she struggled to free herself before twisting and falling off the edge of her bed, toward the ground next to him. Lewis's reaction time was just quick enough to dive his body under hers and break her fall, catching her shoulders and head to his chest before her legs crashed onto the floor. The coolness of her tears hit his bare skin like bullets.

"I'm sorry for waking you," Lewis said as he laid there with her in his arms. "I didn't mean to scare you. I just…you were crying in your sleep, and I wanted to make sure you were okay," he continued, brushing the hair from her face and tracing the outline of her jaw with the pad of his thumb.

"Sorry… I'm okay," Taryn said slowly, staring blankly as if she were trying to convince herself that she was okay, more than trying to convince Lewis.

"You can't lie to me, Ti," Lewis said gently as he tilted her chin up to look at him.

Suddenly, Taryn broke down crying, curling her body around his waist and clenching onto his chest as if it were the only thing holding her to the earth. Her entire body was shaking, and all he could do was pull her closer and hold her until she got it all out. Rocking back and forth with her in his lap, he let her tears drench his skin, making his tattoos glisten each time the moonlight found them in the darkness of her room. His cheek was resting on the top of her head.

"Shhhh. It's okay, Ti. Just let it out. I got you," Lewis repeated over and over again until her body went still.

"I'm so sorry," she said as she pulled away from his chest, looking at him with broken eyes. "I have held it together for over a year now, always doing the right thing for everyone else, thinking if I could get through it, I could put the Toby mess behind me and just focus on trying to be happy again. Now I just…it's too much." She sighed, hanging her head.

"Ti, you don't have to go through this alone. You have your family, Jazzy, Nathan, your parents, and…you have me. So for once in your life, will you let someone else be strong for you?" Lewis reasoned.

"How? I'm the one that is always strong and holding it together for everyone else. If I can't hold it together, what use am I to the people I care about?" Taryn countered.

"You don't always have to hold it together. You're human. You're allowed to fall apart every once in a while, and with everything you've been through this year, let alone the last forty-eight hours, you have every right to," he replied.

"How do you always know how to say the right thing?" Taryn said with a chuckle through her tears as she collapsed back into his chest, wrapping her arms around his waist and snuggling her face into his neck.

"I don't. Sometimes I don't know what to say at all," Lewis said honestly. "But with you, in this situation specifically, you just need to be reminded that no matter how superhuman you are, it's okay for you to be a normal human being sometimes," he joked.

"I guess," Taryn said with a giggle as she sat up again, looking Lewis in his eyes.

"Well, I know." Lewis winked at her.

"Aye! I'm so sorry. Look at you," Taryn said suddenly, reaching for a blanket and wiping his chest gently. "I got all my tears and snot on you. So embarrassing! I'm sorry," she continued, trying to clean him up as they sat there in each other's arms on the floor.

"It's okay," he said, taking her hands in his and stopping her with a kind smile. "My chest is here for you to cry snot onto anytime."

Unable to say anything else, Taryn leaned forward and kissed Lewis gently on the cheek before throwing her arms around his neck and giving him a hug. Lewis wrapped his arms around her waist, squeezing her back. Peeling her from his body, he got up and pulled her up from the ground with him.

"Come on. Back to bed," he said, picking up her blankets and tossing them at the foot of her mattress.

Taryn climbed in willingly as she nuzzled her face into her pillow and pulled a blanket up around her waist.

"Good night," Lewis said, turning to leave.

"Wait," Taryn blurted.

"You need something else?" Lewis asked, hesitating in the doorway.

"Can you stay with me?" Taryn said, unsure of herself. "Like in here?" She patted the empty side of the bed next to her.

"I don't know if that's a good idea, Ti," Lewis replied, reluctantly taking a step back.

"Why not?" Taryn asked sadly.

"Ti, you know what used to happen when you and I would end up lying in a bed together," Lewis retorted bluntly.

"It didn't happen all the time," Taryn argued, sitting up.

"Yes, it did." Lewis laughed. "Unless you were on your period or you fell asleep on your textbooks."

"See, so it wasn't all the time," Taryn joked. "Come on, please? For old times' sake? I just need a cuddle. I promise I'll behave myself," she added as she stuck out her plump lower lip.

"Fine," he said on a heavy sigh. "But just a cuddle. I don't need another baby mama," he teased with a wink as he climbed into bed next to her.

It was as if it were muscle memory for them to be together. Taryn's body instinctively scooted back into his until every inch of her was squished up against his front side. Lewis bent his arm and snaked it under her head for a pillow while his other rested seamlessly wrapped across her waist, his large palm holding her securely to his body. Their knees bent up together, her legs forming to his. It was perfect.

"Good night." Taryn sighed as she nuzzled his arm and let her body melt into his.

"Good night," Lewis replied, kissing her head.

Cradled in each other's bodies, sleep took Lewis and Taryn quickly, as if they only needed to be with each other to find peace.

9

Taryn

Taryn woke up Saturday morning, her eyes puffy and swollen from all the crying. Her heart still ached from everything she had been put through in the last forty-eight hours. Despite this, she woke up smiling and feeling at peace as she lay wrapped up in Lewis's arms. They didn't have to do anything sexually physical with one another, but to have him there with her restored a sense of comfort she lost when they stopped talking ten years ago.

She slowly fidgeted, her body starting to come alive. She tried to savor the last few moments she might have snuggled up to Lewis. The warmth of his breath on her neck, the softness of his skin on hers, and the beat of his heart in his chest against her back was something she realized she had taken for granted all those years ago when they'd hang out.

Taryn arched her back to stretch, and her behind inadvertently rubbed up against Lewis's crotch, prompting his morning wood to grow even harder and protrude beneath his shorts. Taryn's eyes grew wide, and her heartbeat began to quicken as his cock was suddenly fully erect, shoved up against her. Taryn maneuvered in Lewis's arms so she could turn to face him. She had to see the look in his eyes when he realized his body was awake before him. His hardness was now pressed against her tummy.

"Good morning," she said, kissing Lewis on the nose.

"Good morning," he replied sleepily, opening his eyes slowly.

"Still not a morning person, huh?" Taryn replied.

"Not on the weekends." He sighed, rewrapping his arms around her, pulling her close. "It's too early. One more hour."

"I would say okay, but I think Lewis Jr. has other plans in mind." Taryn giggled as she glanced down.

Suddenly aware of his entire self, Lewis shot up in bed, and this time, he was the one tangled and falling over the side. Taryn sat up and laughed as she looked over the edge of her bed at a disheveled Lewis lying on the floor, trying to pull the blankets up around his waist in embarrassment.

"Why are you freaking out?" Taryn laughed. "It's fine. I know it's just the morning thing, you know."

"Ti, I'm trying to be here for you as a friend. I don't want you to think that I'm trying to take advantage of you because you're vulnerable. I can't control him in the morning," Lewis explained through his stuttering, referencing the bulge in his shorts.

"I guess it's my fault. I should've given you the basketball shorts with the built-in underwear." She laughed.

"It's a little late for that now," Lewis joked.

Ding-dong.

The sound of the doorbell broke through their laughter and sent the room into complete silence.

"Who the fuck is that?" Taryn said, worried.

"Jazzy, maybe?" Lewis reasoned.

"No, Jazzy knows the code for the garage door and can come right in. I don't pick up my parents until tomorrow, and all my mom's siblings have their own keys to get in," Taryn replied nervously.

"You have Ring, right? Why don't you check the doorbell camera?" Lewis reminded her.

Reaching for her phone, Taryn pulled up the Ring app to check the doorbell camera as Lewis suggested. Lewis climbed back into bed next to her, cuddling close to see who was ringing her doorbell at seven in the morning on a Saturday. Both of their breathing became heavy, Taryn's from her nerves and Lewis's from his impending anger. It was Toby.

"This fucker has some nerve just showing up here after what he dumped on you last night," Lewis seethed.

"What could he possibly want now? I've given him everything he could want—a divorce, playing the bad guy in that divorce, giving his mom her last wish for me to go see her. I don't know what else he could want! I can't do this right now." Taryn dropped her phone to the bed. Her hands shot up in a feeble attempt to massage some peace back into her temples.

"Stay here. I'll talk to him," Lewis said, getting up.

Man, was Lewis a sight to see. His six-foot frame seemed even taller as he straightened his back out and adjusted the basketball shorts to rest low on his hips. The V-cut from his abs created a perfect arrow to point down to the bulge in his shorts. He wasn't even hard anymore, but you could still see Lewis Jr. like he was ready to hammer someone on the head. He rolled his shoulders, and the muscles in Lewis's back and arms began to tense, his tattoos making him look even more intimidating.

"Lewis," Taryn called, her mind suddenly coming back to life. "Stop. Ignore him and maybe he'll go away."

"Ti, don't worry. I'm just going to talk to him," Lewis replied angrily, already out of her bedroom door.

Getting up quickly, Taryn followed him to the front door. She didn't want to see Toby or vice versa, but she had to be there to keep Lewis in check. If he began to go off and his temper got the best of him, Lewis would pummel Toby. Hiding behind the door, she nodded to Lewis to open it.

"Can I help you?" Lewis said in a gruff voice.

Through the crack where the door met the wall, Taryn could see the shock on Toby's face as he looked up at Lewis, who was towering over him, anger clearly radiating from his body.

"Um, is Taryn home?" Toby asked meekly.

"Why? What do you want? Don't you think you put her through enough already?" Lewis said shortly.

"She told you everything, huh?" Toby said, sighing. "I didn't realize she told her family the truth too already."

53

"She hasn't told her family anything aside from Nathan and Jazzy knowing. She's actually kept to her promise, to take the blame for your fuckups," Lewis fired back at him.

"Oh. How do you know that?" Toby questioned.

"What the fuck does it matter?" Lewis said angrily.

"You're right. It doesn't," Toby agreed, putting his hands up to show he surrendered. "I do need to talk to her though, please. I was serious when I asked her to be the godmother for my daughter, and I actually have one more favor to ask."

"You have no right to ask her of anything else! You think she'd agree to be the godmother of the child conceived by her ex-husband and the slut he cheated on her with? Are you mental?" Lewis said through clenched teeth, his chest beginning to heave in rage and his fists balling at his sides.

Taryn reached her hand out from behind the door and rubbed his back, letting him know she was there, silently pleading for him to calm down. Lewis stood there, taking deep angry breaths as Toby just stood there in shock with wide eyes.

"Look, whether it's asking her to be the godmother or whatever fucked up favor you want from her, she owes you nothing. So leave her alone already and deal with your fuckups by yourself," Lewis said as he slammed the door in Toby's face.

"My mom wanted her to record the song she wrote for her for Mother's Day. To play at the funeral," Toby said loudly through the door in one last attempt to be heard.

Without thinking, Taryn shoved past Lewis and opened the door. Lewis's arm shot out, protectively wrapping around her as Toby's sullen face came into view.

"Trisha put it in her will, that one of the requests for her funeral was to play the song you wrote for her for Mother's Day. She framed the lyrics but could never find anyone to play the chords or sing it the way you did for her. Please, Taryn. Just this last thing, and I promise after this, I'll leave you alone. It would mean the world to her. Don't do it for me. Do it for her. Please," Toby pleaded.

"Fine," Taryn said with a huff. "When I'm done, I'll email it to you. After that, please let me move on with my life."

"I promise. Thank you, Ti," Toby said as he turned to leave.

After shutting the door, Taryn leaned back against the wood and slumped down to the floor, trying to steady her breathing. Lewis squatted down in front of her and took her face in his hands.

"You are so amazing," Lewis said simply as he smiled down at her. "Let's go get some breakfast before we head to my dad's, okay? They're doing the block barbecue with your family today."

She nodded and reluctantly let Lewis pull her up from the ground. They headed into her bathroom to get ready. Her breathing was not stabilized yet, and her knees felt weak, but slowly, with Lewis by her side, she was able to pull herself together.

10

Nathan

Nathan, Sienna, Noah, and Tiana were on their way to have lunch at Pier 39. The plan was to eat some fish-and-chips, beignets, and chowder before walking around the shops. Tiana insisted on also stopping at the Krispy Kreme as well to get some doughnuts to bring home since there wasn't one where they were from. As they entered the restaurant, Nathan's phone started to ring in his pocket. It was Taryn.

"I'll be in there in a few. It's work," Nathan lied as he went to an opening on the dock just behind the restaurant to take the call.

"Good morning, Nate." Taryn's voice sounded cheery over the phone.

"You okay? What the fuck is going on with you? What happened last night?" Nathan cut straight to the chase.

"I'm okay now. Toby's mom had cancer, and I went to see her the day after I got back. Then a few hours after I went to see her, she passed. Being at the hospital and facing everyone was hard enough as it is. Having them overhear Toby break down, all of them hearing what actually happened, made facing them on my way out even harder. It was too much for one day," Taryn shared.

"Okay. So what is this though that Toby wants you to be the godmother to his kid?" Nathan questioned angrily.

"Oh, there was that too. I haven't talked to Toby about that, but I basically blasted him for even considering it through text and told him he was insane," Taryn replied.

"Okay, so you all right then? Like for real?" Nathan asked.

"Yeah. I think so," Taryn stated slowly. "Oh, Toby did show up at the house this morning, asking me to record the Mother's Day song I wrote for Trisha a couple of years ago for them to play at her funeral. I said I would if he left me alone after that. We kinda came to a mutual agreement. It was hard for Toby to push anything more with Lewis's scary ass towering over him."

"Wait, that's right. Lewis called me yesterday. So he's there? Like the Lewis that lived next to Uncle? The Lewis you had feelings for but knew he couldn't commit, so you just fucked around with him until you met Toby? That is the Lewis that is staying with you right now?" Nathan questioned sarcastically.

"Wow...that was such a long time ago, Nate. Seriously, we're just friends," Taryn retorted.

"Uh-huh. Someone who is just a friend doesn't drop their life and fly across an ocean to make sure the other friend is okay. When you are really just friends, you pick up the damn phone to call instead," Nathan mocked.

Taryn grew quiet on the other end of the line.

"Sorry, Ti. I'm just saying. Be careful. You may see him as a friend, but if he didn't have feelings for you still after all these years, he wouldn't have come all the way to Hawai'i just to make sure you're okay," Nathan explained.

"He doesn't have feelings for me," Taryn denied.

"Ti, I know you're like a textbook genius, but you're kinda dumb sometimes," Nathan argued. "You didn't see it ten years ago, and you still don't see it now. I was just a kid, and I could tell he had feelings for you, beyond just being a friend."

"We are just friends," Taryn emphasized again.

"All right, whatever you say," Nathan replied, frustrated.

"I'll call you from Uncle's house later. They're doing their start-of-summer barbecue block party, so I'm going to head there with Lewis in a few hours," Taryn replied.

"Okay. Talk to you later," Nathan said, hanging up the phone.

He loved his sister to death, and she was always hyperaware of the feelings of people around her. For example, if they were sad, she could pick up on it instantly and know exactly what to do to make them smile again. But when it came to picking up on how people felt about her, intimately, she was oblivious, and she was more so blind to her own feelings, pushing how she truly felt deep down inside of her as a means to keep herself from getting hurt. Everyone knew that Lewis and Taryn had mutual feelings for one another growing up, but neither of them had the guts to say anything, and they both were in denial that the other felt the same way. It was so frustrating!

"Everything okay?" Tiana asked as Nathan approached their table, shoving his phone in his pocket with a sigh.

"Yeah, some people are just stupid," he replied, making his reference as general as possible while thinking of his sister.

11

Lewis

It had been years since Lewis took a nice nap after breakfast. They had run through McDonald's and snuggled up on the couch to watch some television before getting ready for the barbeque when they both fell asleep. It was a long night for both of them, and the exhaustion was clear in their bodies.

Laying there, holding Taryn in his arms again as the television watched them, Lewis couldn't help but smile to himself. He took a deep breath of her in so he could savor this moment even longer. Having her with him just felt so right, and despite missing his daughter terribly, he felt happy being by Taryn's side again.

His mind began drifting, imagining what life would have been like for the both of them if he just told her how he felt ten years ago. It was as if they were dating and committed to each other for the entire year, before she met Toby, without actually having a title to define what they were. If he was man enough to tell her how he felt about her, maybe he would have been able to be lucky enough wake up next to her every morning. Maybe she would have been Kam's mom and they'd be together, their own little happy family. Maybe he would have stayed in Hawai'i and gotten everything he'd ever wanted.

The maybes began to sadden him because he knew the man he was ten years ago would have purposely messed up any chance they would have had at a happy life together. He always felt as if he would never be good enough for someone so amazing. Add to that the fact that they were both still immature. It would have been a disaster. The only reason he somewhat committed himself to her for the year, even without being official, was because he didn't want to disrespect her family by sleeping around with other people while being intimate with her.

It was an ironic contradiction that could have been enough to structure his life, to the point he wouldn't mess things up with her. But it wasn't the right timing for them, and he knew they both needed to grow up. He more so cherished her friendship and didn't want to make it official and risk losing her altogether in his life if something went wrong. She was too important to him. Yet he lost her anyways when Toby came along, so what was the point of it all?

"Hmmm." Taryn sighed as she shifted in his arms so she was facing him, the front of their bodies pressed into one another. "You ready to get up?" she said with her eyes still closed.

"Not just yet," he said softly, smiling at her. He pulled her closer into his arms and kissed her forehead. "Fifteen more minutes."

"Okay," she replied as she dropped her head to his chest and nuzzled her way up to his neck.

He squeezed her to him, and Lewis didn't want that moment to end. He wanted to stay like that forever, to protect her, come home to her…to love her. Thinking of her being in the bay with him this summer, even as his professor, he smiled with hope.

"Lewis?" Taryn's breath tickled his neck.

"Hmmm," he replied.

"Lewis Jr. is waking up." She started giggling against his chest, the movement of her body waking him up further as her front rubbed on him.

"Sorry," he said. "I can't control him sometimes."

"It's okay. We gotta get up anyways," she said, giving him one last squeeze. "Don't you have to call Elaine too? Check in on Kam? I'm sure she misses her daddy."

"Fuck, I was supposed to FaceTime them half an hour ago," Lewis said, sitting up quickly as Taryn rolled off his chest and onto the ground. "Damn, I'm sorry, Ti!"

Lewis reached a hand down to her, but she brushed him away, laughing to herself. She was so clumsy, falling all over the place all the time, it never even fazed her anymore.

"I'm good! Go call your daughter." Taryn smiled as she lay on the floor, giving Lewis's behind a smack as he got up.

As Taryn headed to her room, Lewis threw on the hoodie he had shed to the floor the night before. He propped open his iPad and dialed Kam's iPad email that he had set up for her at Christmas.

"Daddy!" Kam's tiny voice echoed through the speakers as she smiled at him from her car seat.

"Hey, Kamy girl! Sorry Daddy is calling a little late. I had some stuff I had to take care of this morning," Lewis replied.

"It's okay, Daddy. I miss you." She smiled.

"I miss you too. I'll be home tomorrow, okay?" Lewis said to his daughter.

"Hey, Lewis? Is everything okay over there?" Elaine's voice echoed in the background. Even if they weren't together, she still cared and worried about him as a friend.

"Yeah. Just some family drama. I'll talk to you about it tomorrow when I pick Kam up," Lewis said.

"Okay. Let me know if you need to stay there longer. Deal with whatever you have to deal with, and I'll hold it down on my end," Elaine replied.

"Thanks. I appreciate that," Lewis told her gratefully. "Is there anything I can bring you guys? Hawai'i snacks or whatever you need me to get?"

"Can you bring me Papa?" Kam asked with big eyes and a smile.

"I wish I could, sweetie, but Papa will come up to visit us later, okay?" Lewis tried to reason with his daughter.

"Oh-kay." She sighed heavily.

"Are you going to the Bay Aquarium toady?" Lewis asked her, trying to change the subject and get her smiling again.

"Yeah!" she exclaimed happily. "I think we're here already, Daddy."

"Yes, we are. Tell Daddy we'll take lots of pictures for him and call him later tonight," Elaine instructed her daughter.

"We gotta go, Daddy. Call you tonight. We'll take lots of pictures," Kam said seriously, echoing her mom.

"Okay." Lewis laughed. "Have fun. Thanks again, Elaine."

"No problem," Elaine replied. "Keep us posted."

"Yeah, keep us posted," Kam chimed.

"I will. Have fun. Bye, you guys. I love you!" Lewis said.

"Bye!" Kam and Elaine said in unison as they hung up the video call, and Lewis's iPad screen went black.

*****

Lewis headed to Taryn's room to see if she was ready yet. As he entered, she was just putting on a tank top. Her pink silk bra on her light cream skin made his heart pound in his chest and blood shoot straight down to his crotch. He swallowed heavily as she tugged at the bottom of her tank top and turned to him standing in the doorway.

"Hey, Lew, should I bring a jacket?" Taryn asked.

She was wearing torn blue denim shorts, a white tank top, and she had white socks on. Her long brown hair fell over her shoulders, the waves from her rubber band causing it to look like ripples in the water. Taryn had put a little makeup on, shading in the outer edges of her eyebrows and putting on some mascara and blush. She used just some Chapstick, and her lips were already full. Her naturally pink, rosy color made her not need lipstick or liner at all. She was breathtaking, and Lewis couldn't help but stare.

"Earth to Lewie?" Taryn said with a frown. "You okay?"

"Fuck...yeah. I'm good. What did you ask?" Lewis replied, aware of the bulge growing in his pants as he tried to hide himself behind the frame of her door.

"I asked if you think I should bring a jacket," Taryn replied with a laugh.

"Definitely. We're meeting the boys after," Lewis stated.

"At town center?" Taryn said excitedly.

"Yeah, Tyson and Kyle planned it. They said since I was home, we gotta all hang out once since it'll be the first time we're all together in a while," Lewis explained.

"I'm excited! That'll be so fun. I haven't seen everyone in forever," Taryn said.

"Well, they're looking forward to it." He smiled.

"What are we waiting for then? Let's go get this day started!" Taryn said, clapping her hands.

Lewis was happy to see Taryn excited to meet up with all their old friends, like old times, but he was nervous. He could only imagine the crap that would happen. He could see their friend Paul trying to hit on her now that she's single again; Kyle, drunk, trying to instigate something between Lewis and Taryn; or his friend Thomas, joking too harshly with her too soon about the divorce. He loved his friends, but they had no boundaries with one another, and unfortunately, because of that, they knew no boundaries with Taryn, sometimes coming off extremely inappropriate. Even if she was used to it and Taryn was more than capable of handling herself, Lewis knew it was going to be a long night.

12

Derek

He sat in his trailer between takes and held the orange-wrapped candy left behind from Taryn in his hand. Sighing to himself, he couldn't stop thinking about her. About everything she was going through, about wanting to be with her, about this Lewis guy that was being her knight in shining armor right now when he wanted to be that guy for her. Derek's mind was completely consumed with thoughts of Taryn.

"You okay?" Ben asked as he, Jared, and Ananya opened his trailer door and let themselves in.

"Yeah. I'm fine," Derek said with a fake smile, missing his signature eye twinkle.

"Liar," Ananya said. "I know we play love interests in the series, but in reality, you're like the big brother I never had. I hate seeing you like this."

"She's right," Jared added. "Why are you sitting here moping over her? Why don't you just call her or text her, at least?"

"What harm could it do?" Ben finished.

"Guys, I'm okay." Derek sighed as his gaze dropped to the floor. "I can't call her or text her. I think she blocked me. And besides, she has too much going on right now for me to try and talk to her. For me to want to do that, to figure things out between us when she's going through so much back home is just…selfish. I can't do that to her. She just needs time."

"Maybe she needs to hear from you too. She's waiting for you to comfort her and show you're there for her through whatever she's dealing with, and you're just being too stupid to try," Ananya argued.

"She already has someone helping her. It's too late. And like I said, I think she blocked me," Derek said, his heart sinking.

"What do you mean, bro?" Ben asked.

"Lewis…her friend Lewis? The one from the restaurant. He flew to Hawai'i to be by her side when he found out everything that was going on. They have history together. He found her when she disappeared the other night, and he's been staying at her house with her," Derek retorted.

"The Lewis guy that we saw at K-Elements?" Jared asked to clarify.

"Yes, that Lewis. The muscular tattooed monster of a guy," Derek said, his voice tinged in jealousy.

"Huh! This is why girls get so frustrated with you men!" Ananya said, stalking over to his vanity and yanking the bottom drawer open and pulling out the letter Taryn had left Derek.

"How did you know that was in there?" Derek asked defensively as she stalked toward him.

"I may or may not go through your guys' stuff for fun and to look to prank you sometimes," she said guilty. "But that's not important! What's important is that Taryn said she loves you."

Ananya shoved the letter into Derek's chest and pointed hard at the line where Taryn had confessed her feelings toward Derek. Everyone was shocked.

"She loves *you*, Derek," Ananya repeated.

"If she did, she wouldn't have blocked me. She would've talked to me by now and let me explain myself," Derek argued.

"Let me paint you a picture because you obviously don't get it from a girl's perspective," Ananya seethed. "Taryn wrote you this letter to prevent herself from getting hurt. You said her ex-husband that she was with for eight or nine years cheated on her. That shit probably fucked her up to the point she felt like she wasn't good enough for anyone already. Then after finally falling for someone else, she sees your dumb ass kiss Lexie, *confirming* her belief about herself. She ran from you because she's afraid to get hurt. Now flash forward to whatever crap she's going through in Hawai'i, trying to reopen her heart to potentially get hurt by you again, Derek, is probably the *last* thing on her mind right now. The fact that you haven't so much as called her or sent her a text since her brother told you she flew home, in her mind, it just shows you never really cared about her to begin with. And to top it off, if she really did block you, like the lame excuse you're trying to use, none of your messages to her would have even been marked as delivered."

Derek sat back in his chair, trying to take it all in. His mind was racing, and he felt like the biggest idiot.

"So," Ananya continued, "you need to get off your high horse and fucking call her. If you don't, I hope this Lewis guy sweeps her off her feet and steals her from you because you aren't even fighting to keep her in your life at this point."

"Damn, Anya, that's brutal," Ben chimed.

"The truth hurts sometimes, sweetheart. Deal with it," Ananya replied sarcastically.

"She's right, Derek," Jared said with a sigh.

"Derek, we all care about you, and we hate seeing you so bummed about Taryn. But here's some tough love, okay? If you don't do something about the situation you got yourself into, you can't mope around playing the victim," Ananya added before giving him a hug. "Please stop being a dummy and text her. You got about fifteen minutes until we need you for the next scene, so hurry it up."

With that, the three of them left Derek in his trailer with his thoughts. Ananya was right. He had to do something to show that he truly cared about Taryn. But what gesture to make so she'd talk to him, he didn't know. Pulling out his phone, he decided to text her the one thing he'd been wanting to say to her since he realized how he truly felt.

"I love you Taryn." (Derek)

Before he could think twice about what he just texted, he hit Send. After seeing that it was delivered, he placed his phone down on the vanity counter and took a deep breath, hoping that would at least get her talking to him, regardless if she was mad or happy at him about it. He would rather have her cussing him out than ignoring him altogether at this point.

13

Lewis

The annual start of summer barbecue block party that Lewis's dad and Taryn's uncle would host was an event to look forward to. Everyone brought tons of food, potluck style, and they would be barbecuing and smoking meat a week in advance to prepare. Lewis hadn't been to one of these since he moved up to California. It felt so good to be home and hang out with everyone.

With a Heineken in hand, he sat back in the lawn chair and watched the scene before him. The kids playing, the men at the grill, and the women scattered about helping everyone in whatever way they could. Taryn was helping Jazzy refill the blow-up pool for the kids. One of the kids didn't realize they couldn't sit on the wall of the pool, and it caused a tidal wave down the driveway. It was hilarious to see the aunties scurry to try and catch the kids while the kids were all yelling, unsure of what was happening. Lewis smiled at Taryn, thinking how awesome she was with all the little ones despite not being a mom herself.

"Daydreaming there?" Taryn's cousin Chaz said as he sat on a chair next to Lewis.

"Nah, just observing. Enjoying the moment while we here, right?" Lewis said gratefully.

"So what's up with you and Ti?" Chaz asked casually, nodding toward his cousin.

When they pulled up to the barbecue, Lewis's entire family was surprised that he was home. But what was even more surprising to everyone was that he came home with Taryn.

"Nothing…just chillin'," Lewis replied.

"Right," Chaz said, swigging his beer. "Just take care of her, all right? She's already been through enough."

"I promise I'll take care of her, but it's not like that. We're just friends," Lewis emphasized.

"Stop lying to yourself, Lewie-boy," Chaz teased, shaking his head and giving Lewis a hard pat on the shoulder as he got up and walked away.

Chaz was two years older than Taryn, but their birthdays were mere days apart, so their families would always combine birthday parties since they were little. Being Chaz's neighbor, Lewis and his family would always be invited, and he literally saw them grow up together. Although Chaz always played the role of being the laid-back cousin, he was extremely protective of Taryn, even if he never said it aloud to anyone. Back when he found out that Taryn and Lewis were getting close, he threatened to stomp on Lewis's wind-pipe if he ever hurt Taryn. Of course, no one knew about this, but Lewis understood where Chaz was coming from and respected him even more so for it. In Hawai'i, you protect your own. Taryn's phone suddenly buzzed in her purse that Lewis was watching.

"Ti, your phone," Lewis called out to her as he pulled her phone from her bag.

Inadvertently, Lewis looked down at the screen and caught a glimpse of the text message she had received.

"I love you Taryn." (Derek)

Despite telling himself over and over again that they were just friends, that he couldn't cross that line and confess to her how he felt because he didn't want to lose her as a friend, seeing the text message from this Derek dude hurt. Lewis began to feel uncomfortable.

"Who is it?" Taryn asked nonchalantly with a smile as she approached Lewis.

"I think it's better if you check it yourself," Lewis said, handing Taryn the phone as he got up and walked away from her.

"Lew?" Taryn called after him, unsure why his mood suddenly changed. "Lewis!"

He had to get away from her and clear his head. He took a walk to the neighborhood park about ten minutes away. Maybe he read the message wrong? Maybe it was one of her gay cheer friends? Lewis tried to find reason within his mind that could explain that text and restore the hope that sparked these last few days, the hope that said maybe one day he and Taryn could be together. But he knew it wouldn't happen. It wasn't meant to be ten years ago, and it wasn't meant to be now. Regardless of how he felt about her, at the end of the day, he was just her friend.

14

Taryn

"What's going on?" Jazzy asked, approaching Taryn as Lewis seemingly stormed off after handing over her phone.

"I don't know," Taryn said, confused.

Lewis had been her rock the last twenty-four hours, and everything was going wonderfully with him back in her life. He was the comfort she was missing this past year. But she didn't know what she could have done to get him so upset at her all of a sudden.

"Did he say anything?" Jazzy questioned.

"He just told me to check my phone," Taryn said, looking down at the device in her hand.

She tapped the screen to turn it on, and her breath seemed to constrict in her throat as she saw Derek's name pop up. His text message was loud and clear beneath it.

"I love you Taryn." (Derek)

"Who the fuck is Derek?" Jazzy questioned suspiciously.

"He's just a guy from San Fran," Taryn tried to play it off.

"Well, 'just a guy' seems to love you. So what truth are you not telling me now?" Jazzy spat.

"He's Nathan's friend's older brother. We got close when I was up there. It all happened really fast," Taryn said guiltily.

"Like got to know each other really fast or like you slept with him already fast?" Jazzy scolded.

"Both?" Taryn replied, hanging her head. "He was going through a similar fucked-up relationship situation, and we kinda took comfort in each other. It just happened."

"Jeez, Ti! What are you thinking? You don't even know this guy, and you're spilling your guts to him while spreading your legs?" Jazzy seethed.

"Don't judge me, okay! After the year I had, I was bound to go off the deep end sooner or later. And yes, I spilled everything to him, specifically because he didn't know me! He had no judgment of me. He just listened! Fuck!" Taryn snapped.

The entire party fell silent. All eyes were glued on Taryn.

"I have to go find Lewis and explain everything to him. I can't have you disappointed in me, with him being mad at me, on top of Toby's shit, and now Derek's apparently," Taryn said, storming off.

Just as Lewis knew Taryn to a tee, she knew Lewis. So she headed for the park. When they were growing up and he would get into fights with his dad, he would spend hours at the park, just sitting on the swings to clear his head. She ripped into the parking lot with her car. He was exactly where she knew he'd be. She got out and walked over to him.

"I guess we should talk?" Taryn said with a heavy sigh.

"It's okay. Don't worry about it," Lewis replied coldly without lifting his head to look at her.

"No, it's not okay," Taryn said, taking a seat on the swing next to him. "Lewis, you mean the world to me. You're one of my closest friends. I can't have you mad at me, not when I just got you back in my life."

"Close friends?" Lewis questioned. "Taryn, you have no idea, do you? How I felt about you? How I feel?"

Lewis was becoming increasingly frustrated.

"Fine. Then why don't you tell me!" Taryn retorted.

"Ti... I... I've always..." Lewis sighed, unable to finish his sentence. "It's never going to be me and you, is it?"

"Lewis, I—" Taryn tried to begin.

"No, let me finish. I have to get this off my chest." Lewis cut her off. "Taryn, that year we spent together was the best year of my life. Even if we were never official, in my head you were my girl, and I would've stayed committed to you. Then Toby came along and suddenly, it was as if everything I thought we had was just a delusion in my head. Like I was just someone to occupy your time while you waited for Mr. Right to come along and sweep you off your feet."

Taryn was stunned into silence. Her heart crumbled in her chest after hearing Lewis's revelation. She had no idea he saw her as anything more than his neighbor's dorky cousin and someone to hook up with on occasion. Everyone always told her he liked her and to be patient with him, but after a year of waiting for him to be upfront with her about how he felt, she figured she was hoping for something that would never happen. She figured she would call it like it seemed, that they were just fuck buddies. Never in a million years could she had guessed he felt this way. He was such an amazing guy beyond what façade he put out for the rest of the world to see. The thought that she had hurt him killed her inside.

"Lewis, I'm so sorry. After a year, I thought I was the one imagining things," Taryn choked out softly, unsure of what else to even say.

"Don't be sorry. It was my fault I couldn't man up enough to be honest with you about how I felt. I'm the one that should be sorry for pulling back from our friendship. Seeing you with Toby crushed me, and it was too difficult to just be your friend at that point. When you see the person you love happy with someone else, a part of your heart dies," Lewis said sadly.

"That's my karma, I guess. I know the feeling," Taryn said, thinking about her divorce and the situation with Toby. "Lewis, why didn't you just tell me?"

"If I'm being honest, it's because I was scared you wouldn't feel the same way. Ti, you're amazing. You're talented, athletic, smart, you have the whole world going for you. With my reputation and bad judgment at the time, I knew I could never be good enough for you," Lewis replied sadly.

"Lewis! Don't say that! Don't you ever put yourself down! You are the sweetest, most loyal, and caring person I know. Any girl would be lucky to have you," Taryn argued.

"Well… I was also scared to fuck things up. I still had that young boy mindset, and we both needed to mature, you know? I didn't want to risk messing things up with you then because I couldn't control my dick around you and end up losing you in my life altogether. I'd rather have you as a friend than nothing at all," Lewis admitted as he rested a hand on her knee.

"I get it." Taryn sighed. "I'm still sorry though."

"Why?" Lewis questioned.

"Because maybe if I told you how I felt, it would've changed your mind," Taryn said.

"Nah, I still would've run," Lewis said jokingly.

"So you bolted from the barbecue today because I'm assuming you saw Derek's text?" Taryn asked.

"Yep. See? I'm a runner." Lewis nodded as he began pushing the swing softly. "Gave me flashbacks that I wasn't ready to face just yet. Still processing picking up our friendship again."

"Derek is a guy from San Fran. He's Nathan's—" Taryn sighed as she tried to explain.

"You don't have to explain anything, Ti. You're single. You can talk to whoever you want. It just gave me flashbacks of Toby swooping in like a diseased fly," Lewis interjected, making Taryn giggle at his description.

"Just to clarify though, maybe ease your mind. Derek and I aren't anything. Even if he thinks he feels that way, he'd be crazy to after only meeting me at Nathan's graduation. And he still has a thing with his ex. It's just a big complicated mess," Taryn summed on a sigh.

"Well, he is crazy to tell you that after like a week," Lewis joked. "But seriously, he would be crazier not to fall in love with you. Any guy would have to be an idiot to not have their heart melt at your feet after spending a mere twenty minutes with you, Ti."

"Thanks, I guess." Taryn smiled meekly, shrugging her shoulders.

"I'm serious, Ti. Whoever you end up with better treat you like a queen and never let you go because they'd be lucky to have you in their life…period." Lewis smiled as he gave her hand a squeeze.

Taryn's emotions were all a mess. Derek had showed her this week that for the first time in a year, she could feel happiness and love again. Yet now, with Lewis, she felt the comfort and security that she was missing in her life since they put their friendship on pause ten years ago. She didn't know what to do or how to feel.

"Come on," Lewis said, offering a hand out to her as he stood up. Taryn took it gratefully and allowed him to pull her into his arms and hug her. "Stop overthinking," Lewis said, kissing her forehead.

"Don't tell me what to do." She laughed meekly.

How could she not overthink? She was torn between the fiery passion with Derek and her history with Lewis. She wasn't even ready for a relationship, but she couldn't help the nagging feeling pulling at her heartstrings. Staying in the friend zone with either of them would be difficult, but what would be even more difficult would be hurting someone she cared about. She had already been intimate with Derek, losing herself in moments with him with the strong, magnetic connection they seemed to have. But with Lewis's newfound confession, she felt as if staying as his friend would only add to the pain she already caused him, and she could never do that to him again. Her mind was a mess, and her emotions were even messier. Taryn had to figure shit out, and she had to figure it out quickly before she hurt anyone else.

15

Lewis

After helping to clean up after the barbeque, Lewis stayed at his dad's house to shower and get ready while Taryn used Jazzy's shower to do the same.

"So you and Ti? Are you actually going to go for it and make it official this time? It took you ten years and another guy stealing her away only to break her heart for you to come to your senses?" his older sister Mallory told him as she leaned on the doorframe to his old room.

"Mal, the more I think about it, the more I realize we're meant to just be friends," Lewis said as he used some gel to comb over his hair.

"In what universe?" Mal asked sarcastically.

"Look, if I wasn't good enough for her then, what makes you think she would even want to date a single father? She's been through too much already. I can't throw baby mama drama on her as well. That'd be selfish of me," Lewis argued.

"For once in your life, will you be selfish when it comes to this girl? Last time you were too afraid to disrespect her family and to lose her friendship. Now you don't want to burden her with my amazing niece?" Mal scoffed.

"That's not fair. I never said Kam was a burden. She's the love of my life, if anything," Lewis retorted. "I just don't think it's fair of me to expect Ti to just jump in and be a mom because of my feelings for her."

"Well, I think she'd jump at the opportunity," his sister argued. "Jazzy told me all about her PCOS."

"Wait, what?" Lewis asked, confused.

"I'm guessing by the look on your face, you don't know?" Mal replied, confused. When they spoke earlier, Lewis said Taryn had recently told him everything.

"No, really? I actually know, but I'm just playing stupid," Lewis said sarcastically.

"Well, you are stupid sometimes. You don't gotta pretend," Mallory teased. "But seriously, she has PCOS, polycystic ovary syndrome. It makes it really hard to have kids. There's like a 98 percent chance that women who have it won't ever get pregnant at all. It sucks for Ti because she's always been naturally caring and protective. She would be a great mom."

Lewis plopped onto his bed as he tried to comprehend yet another thing Taryn had been dealing with in secret. Now it all made sense, and he understood now why it hurt her so much to see Toby having kids with Annalee and why it triggered her to have Toby ask her to be the godmother.

"You know that's part of the reason she got divorced, right?" Mal continued. "She was going to stay with Toby until she found out he got that other chick pregnant. She realized that chick could give him the one thing he always wanted but Ti could never give him. So she dipped so he could have his family."

"Wait, how do you know all of this?" Lewis questioned.

"You'll be surprised what comes out with a few glasses of wine and some girl talk," Mal said casually.

"So you guys just spill each other's secrets like that? Girl talk?" Lewis questioned. He would tell his boys stuff, but nothing that personal unless they shared it with the group themselves.

"Yeah. It was about a year ago. When Taryn found out she was diagnosed. She came over to Jazzy's for some girl time and had a complete breakdown. Spilled about the PCOS, how Toby would be better off without her since she couldn't give him kids, then boom!

Next thing we know, she was filing for divorce," Mal explained. "You don't need to be a rocket scientist to put two and two together. So don't count yourself out yet, Lewie."

"Will you stop?" Lewis laughed. "We're just friends, and I don't even know what she would want right now. She's going through a lot. The timing just isn't right."

"The timing will never be right, but okay, I'll lay off," Mal replied, walking backward with her hands up. "But I do like stirring the pot, so I'm hoping I planted a few seeds in your head to consider. We all love Ti, and whether she's a friend or more, she's already like a sister to me. Okay. I'll go now."

With a laugh, Mal left Lewis to his thoughts. His sister was too much sometimes, but despite her crazy ideas, she did have some valid points. He just wished Taryn had told him about her PCOS. How could he be there for her with that if she didn't even tell him? The secret would eat him alive, and he couldn't bring it up to her if she didn't tell him because that meant she didn't want him knowing. This was going to be a long night.

*****

"You ready?" Taryn said, approaching the car.

"Yeah, the guys will—" Lewis stopped.

Taryn's beauty hit him like a bullet train. The gray leggings she wore hugged every curve of her body in just the right places. A simple loose black tank top flowed around her freely with a gold zipper settling between her breasts and exposing a hint of cleavage. On her feet, she had strappy black heels on, and a matching black clip held her hair up in a messy and loose bun with a few of her long brown locks hanging out, framing her face. She had on her rose-gold glasses tonight, giving off that sexy teacher look, the look that could make schoolboys and men alike want to stay after class for detention.

"Wow. You look amazing, Ti," Lewis uttered.

"Thanks. I forgot extra clothes to change into, so I'm just borrowing some from Jazzy." She smiled. "I'm glad the stress didn't make my boobs shrink, or I wouldn't have fit into her bra!"

Taryn laughed, pushing up her cleavage in front of his face with a wink. The motion made Lewis go weak at the knees, and his cock started to throb in his pants.

"Wanna know a secret?" Taryn whispered to him as he walked her around to open her door. "Tonight I'm the one free balling it! I'm fine borrowing Jazzy's clothes but will never borrow someone else's panties, even if they have been washed."

"You're too much, Ti," Lewis said, laughing, looking down at his crotch and trying to talk himself down in his head. "Don't tell that secret to the guys, or I'll have to fight them off all night," he added, walking around to the driver's side.

The ride to town center was a mere ten minutes from the barbecue block party. It felt nice for them to hang out together again, and Lewis was looking forward to seeing all his boys. As they pulled into the parking lot, they found their friends all hanging out, talking around their cars. All of them looked absolutely monstrous. All of their friends, including Tyson, the smallest of the group, stood tall, at least five-ten, with arm and shoulder muscles galore. Each of them had at least one of their arms smothered in various tattoos.

"Here he is!" Paul yelled as he walked over to their car to shake Lewis's hand.

"What's up, Paul?" Lewis said excitedly as he shook his friend's hand and gave him a hug.

"Hello, my lady," Thomas said in his deep, smooth voice as he leaned down to help Taryn out of the car.

"Tommy!" she exclaimed as she tiptoed to give him a hug, the scruff on his face rubbing into the crook of her neck.

"Damn, Ti. Ten years done you good," Paul said, looking at her from across the car. "You're not baby Ti no more. You're all grown up." He laughed to himself.

"Oh, geez. Here we go," Lewis said with a laugh, shaking his head.

"Paul! Give Ti a second to breathe, huh?" Tyson interjected as he approached them. "Hey again, Ti. Paul's corny ass hasn't changed." He turned to Taryn, giving her a hug.

"Not at all." Taryn laughed.

"Wow, so I'm just left out of the greetings? Whatever," Kyle said sarcastically as he stood next to the trunk.

"Of course not! Good to see you again, Kyle," Taryn said, walking over and hugging him too.

"Now that's more like it," Kyle replied.

The six of them walked through the parking lot, joking around and getting honked at by cars like they did ten years ago when Ti was barely out of high school and the boys were in their early twenties. It felt good to be home and around his boys again. When it was guys' night like this, Taryn typically didn't come out with him unless Jazzy and Mal came along too, but he knew she needed a night out, and with him there, he could make sure she was cared for the entire time.

They walked into the Mexican restaurant at the town center, and a waiter approached with two plates of chips and homemade salsa. The Latino music and colorful red and green lights brought a smile to Taryn's face. The waiter placed menus down and went over the specials before asking to take their drink orders.

"Coronas all around," Paul said excitedly as he took out his ID and credit card. "First round is on me! It's good to have our Lewie-boy home!"

Everyone sang out thanks to Paul as the conversation kicked into full gear. Everyone was catching up, sharing all the positives about their lives now, keeping the mood happy and upbeat. Despite the craziness of the past week, Taryn felt happy again.

"So how's our niece doing, Lewie-boy?" Thomas asked as he swigged his beer. "You gotta move home soon so your nephew can meet his future wife."

"Easy does it, Tommy," Kyle said. "Even if it's your kid, Lewis ain't letting Kam get a boyfriend until she's fifty!"

"If she glows up like Ti did over here, she's going to have her first boyfriend before she's fifteen," Paul said with a wink.

"See! You gotta come home! Then Kam will have all her uncles to protect her against any dude that even tries," Tyson urged.

"I know. I miss home," Lewis admitted. "But right now, California is what works for us. Elaine is there too, so Kam is close to both parents. I wouldn't want to put her through anything and take either of us away from her because I'm being selfish. It's just wrong. I can't do that to her."

Taryn saw the sincerity and how torn he was in his eyes. She reached out and gave his knee a gentle squeeze under the table to show she understood and supported him. He was grateful for it, and he rested his hand on hers and gave a little squeeze back.

"So, Ti. Divorced, I heard?" Paul turned his attention to Taryn once again.

"Sadly, yes." She sighed heavily. "But I'm okay. Dealing with it one day at a time and doing much better."

"He didn't deserve you, Ti. You were always too good for him. We all thought so, from the second we found out you were dating him," Tyson interjected some support into the conversation.

"Thanks, Tys," Taryn said with a grateful smile.

"So you're single?" Paul continued.

"Yes." Taryn laughed half-heartedly, shaking her head. She expected nothing less from Paul.

"You going to give my boy a chance or what this time?" Paul added, pointing at Lewis with his beer bottle.

Lewis almost choked on the sip of beer he was taking. He placed the bottle down and coughed. Taryn sat up and began rubbing his back instinctively.

"Dumb ass," Lewis said to Paul, shaking his head.

"What? It's a serious question," Paul retorted. "And if she won't give you a chance, then maybe I have a shot?"

"We're just friends," Taryn said with a smile.

"You and I are just friends? Or you and Lewis are just friends?" Paul questioned with a smirk.

"Both," Taryn said with a laugh.

Lewis shot a daggered glance across the table that pierced through Paul's relaxed exterior. Paul knew not to push any further. Even if they were about the same size, Lewis had heavy hands, and Paul knew not to go toe-to-toe with him. Paul was more of a pretty boy that looked intimidating because of his size, but Lewis had been into so many fights growing up, his fists were lethal.

In their group of friends, it was always Lewis and Kyle that would never back down from a fight, causing them to get suspended multiple times throughout high school. That's why when Lewis joined the Military, everyone was shocked. No one thought he would do well with the structure and discipline. But instead of faltering, he excelled.

After about two more hours of drinking and countless laughs later, everyone closed their tabs and headed toward the parking lot.

"You guys good to drive?" Lewis asked his friends.

"I'm driving these donkeys home. I had just that one that Paul got, so I'm sober already," Tyson said.

"Our little Ty-Wy always so responsible," Kyle said drunkenly, poking Tyson in the cheek.

"On second thought, if this one doesn't get home, it's probably because I left his ass on the side of the road," Tyson replied, glaring at Kyle.

"Bye, Ti! Call you later, bro!" Kyle replied with his hands up in surrender to Tyson as he climbed into the passenger seat.

Thomas was walking with Paul, half holding him up, half dragging him.

"Bye, guys. It was good seeing both of you," Thomas said as he tried to get Paul in the backseat of Tyson's car.

"Wait!" Paul yelled suddenly. "Ti! Come here, pleassee," he slurred.

"Yes?" Ti said as she stood over Paul, his body in the car with his head hanging out.

"I didn't get to tell you goodbye," Paul said sadly.

"Well, goodbye, Paul." Taryn laughed. "I'll see you around, okay?"

"No! That's not a goodbye! You hugged everyone else but me!" Paul whined.

"Okay, I'm sorry, Paul," Taryn said as she bent down to give him a hug.

Suddenly, Paul's hands were wrapped around her waist, and he yanked her down, crashing down his mouth onto hers. Taryn struggled to push him off, pulling her neck back to put space between the two of them. But even in his drunken state, Paul was too strong. He held her, forcing his mouth onto her hers as she was rendered helpless in his hold.

Lewis and Thomas sprang into action. From behind her, Lewis pried Paul's hands apart and yanked Taryn from his grips to safety, trying to use his body as a shield from Paul. From the opposite end of the car, Thomas pulled Paul out from the car and onto the pavement.

"What the fuck are you doing?" Thomas yelled at Paul, who was now slumped against the back tires of Tyson's car.

"I wanted to see if she tasted as good as she looked," Paul slurred.

Lewis was frantic as he turned to Taryn. He held her by her arms and scanned her face for any abrasions. He ran his hands down her arms and lifted her wrists, his eyes covering every inch of her body to make sure she was okay.

"Lewis, I'm okay," Taryn tried to calm him. "It's fine."

Unable to speak, he pulled her into his arms and hugged her protectively, his breath heaving with anger.

"Lewis, I promise I'm fine. Paul's just drunk. It's okay. Let it go," Taryn tried to reason.

Suddenly hearing his name and remembering Paul, anger exploded from him, and his body shook with a rage that slowly started to take over. Seeing the change in his demeanor, Tyson walked up cautiously to Lewis.

"Lewis, calm down. Paul isn't worth it." Tyson tried to talk to Lewis, but it was too late.

Releasing Taryn, he effortlessly maneuvered around Tyson and walked over to where Paul was slumped down. Lewis clenched his fist. He pulled his arm back and, with a loud wallop, swung down full force into Paul's jaw. Or at least what he thought was Paul's jaw.

Taryn's whimpers snapped Lewis out of his state of rage. Blinking to clear his vision, blurred of anger, he saw Paul still sitting there, not a mark on him. Thomas was kneeling next to Taryn, who was now on the ground. Tyson was next to her, holding her head up as Taryn held her face. Blood was dripping from her lips and down her arms.

"What the fuck?" Lewis's voice shook.

"What do *you* mean what the fuck? Lewis, you punched Ti!" Tyson yelled. "What the fuck is wrong with you?"

"Wait...what?" Lewis's eyes filled with fear and remorse.

"She got in between the two of you to try and stop you from hitting Paul. She didn't want you to ruin your friendship with him because of her. You must've blacked out because next thing we know, you swung at her," Thomas summed up.

Lewis dropped to his knees, pieces of the last few seconds flashing back to him—Taryn's brown eyes pleading with him to stop and to calm down, her hands resting on his shoulders, trying to get him to snap out of it. His knuckles connecting with a crunch to her tiny jaw, sending her hair to fly wildly around her face as she fell to the ground.

"Fuck!" Lewis yelled, angry with himself.

His fists met the pavement with frustration, feeling helpless and unsure of what else to do. Thomas and Tyson both watched him warily. Kyle and Paul both passed out, oblivious to what was going on.

"Ti," Lewis said gently. "Are you okay? I'm so sorry."

In a feeble attempt to check on her, he reached out, touching her leg. Taryn flinched under his touch.

"Go grab a towel from my trunk," Tyson instructed him.

Handing the towel to Tyson, Lewis stood, watching helplessly. Tyson was a nurse, so he knew she was in good hands. He hated himself for being the cause of Taryn's pain, and more so for not being able to do anything to help.

"Ti, I'm going to lift your head up a little, okay? I need to check if you hit your head on the pavement. There's a lot of blood, and I want to check to make sure it's not from your head, okay?" Tyson said gently as Taryn's body relaxed so he could move her.

Thomas helped Tyson to turn her, allowing him to brace her body on his forearms as he checked the back of her head.

"Fuck," Tyson said softly. "She has a cut on the back of her head. Probably from falling backward. She might have a concussion."

Tyson and Thomas laid Taryn back down, using the towel as a cushion for her head. Tyson's hands were bright red with her blood. The panic on his face was clearly growing as he thought of what to do next.

"We need to call an ambulance," Tyson said to Lewis.

"Okay, whatever she needs. Just do it," Lewis replied.

"No," Taryn groaned softly as she released her jaw and gingerly sat up. Thomas held her hand and braced her back.

"Ti, you need to go to a hospital," Tyson tried to reason with her gently.

"I'm fine," Taryn argued stubbornly.

"Ti, you have a huge cut on the back of your head, and your jaw could be fractured," Tyson argued.

Lewis's heart dropped, and he felt like the biggest piece of shit just hearing the damage he had caused her so quickly. He wanted to beat himself up.

"My jaw is a little tender, but I've been kicked in the face so many times before for cheer. I'd know if it were fractured, and it's not. It just looks bad because my lip got cut on my teeth," Taryn replied, slowly lifting her hand and pulling her bottom lip down to show a gash in the center.

"But your head, Ti. You need to get checked and at least bandaged up. You shouldn't take a chance with potential concussions," Tyson retorted.

Taryn was silent for a few minutes before sighing heavily.

"Fine. But no ambulance. Riding in them makes me nauseated," she said.

"Thank you, Ti, for listening," Tyson said sweetly. "Lewis, I'll give you another towel. Make sure she's sitting up the whole way there. Keep her awake," he went on to instruct Lewis.

"I'll come with you guys," Thomas said. "I can sit behind her and help to hold her up in case she gets dizzy. That way, you can focus on getting her to the hospital fast, okay?"

"After I drop these clowns off home, I'll come by the ER so I can check on her and take Thomas home. Just text me which one you guys are at," Tyson added as he peeled Paul off the ground and pushed his lifeless body into the backseat.

"Thank you, guys," Lewis said, his voice cracking with emotion.

He and Thomas walked her to the car, climbed in, and let the streetlights guide their way to the hospital.

16

Taryn

Taryn laid in the emergency room bed, a white towel giving extra padding between her head and the pillow. She never understood why they used white when someone was bleeding. It would stain and made things look worse than it was. She sighed as she looked over to Lewis, his hand gripping onto hers, the wetness from his tears apparent on her forearm. His guilt was unbearable for her to watch. It was just an accident.

"Lewis." Taryn sighed, reaching across her body and rubbing the back of his head with her free hand.

"Ti, don't. You're going to tangle your IV," he replied, gently placing her hand back on the other side of the bed.

"It's not your fault," Taryn emphasized gently.

"Yes, it is. If I didn't swing at Paul, I wouldn't have hit you," he retorted, hanging his head.

"It was an accident, Lewis. You were just trying to protect me," Taryn persisted.

"And look how that turned out. I hit you instead, and now we're in the ER. You had to get stitches put in, and you might have a concussion. Don't tell me that's not my fault," Lewis argued.

"For me, will you just stop? Please," she pleaded. "I'm fine. It's not like I've never been rocked like this before."

In all her years of doing competitive club cheer, she had been knocked unconscious, had her eyelid busted open, broken her nose, had her lip cut up, dislocated her shoulder, and torn her meniscus. At one point, she had five concussions within four years. Her doctors were ready to force her to quit, but she refused.

"Ti, this isn't like your cheer injuries." Lewis knew exactly what she was comparing this to.

"Yes, it is. It was an accident. It's no one's fault," she argued. "And if you keep insisting you're to blame, your ass can go sit outside in the waiting room or go home."

Lewis just hung his head and sighed heavily. He wasn't going anywhere, and she knew it. She could tell he wanted to argue back but didn't want to risk getting kicked out of her room.

"Hey, Ti," Tyson said as he knocked on the door. Thomas and Jazzy stood with him.

"Hey." Taryn smiled meekly. "Thank you, Tommy, for helping me in the car, and, Tys, for picking up Jazzy on your way down here."

"Anytime," the two men said in unison.

"So what the fuck happened? You're so fucking clumsy, Ti. It had to be you, of all people, to get hurt and need stitches within a few days of being back home," Jazzy joked.

"It's nothing. It was just an accident." Taryn giggled.

Tyson and Thomas looked cautiously over to Lewis, who was clearly biting his tongue.

"Well, thank you guys for helping this ditz," Jazzy said to the guys as she pulled up a chair to sit on the other side of Taryn. "Lewis, don't look so upset. It's not your job to prevent her from being herself and falling."

"I hit her," Lewis said softly, barely above a whisper.

"What?" Jazzy questioned, unsure if she heard him correctly.

"I said… I hit her," Lewis repeated.

"What the fuck, Lewis?" Jazzy was standing now, the chair flying backward, completely erratic.

"It was an accident," Taryn jumped in. "Paul was drunk, forced me to kiss him, and wouldn't let me go. Lewis was trying to protect me. I got in his way to stop him from killing Paul, and the timing was just off. It was an accident."

"Fuck. Okay." Jazzy tried to process, catching her breath, trying to calm herself. "You blanked out again, didn't you? I thought you had that anger shit under control, Lewis?"

"I do, or I did. I just blanked when I saw what Paul did. I'm sorry." Lewis sighed, hanging his head and sobbing.

"We're going to wait outside," Tyson said, grabbing Thomas's arm to follow him.

"Lewis, it's okay. You were trying to protect her. No one told her dumb ass to jump in front of you when you were already swinging. It was an accident. Stop blaming yourself for something that's done already," Jazzy tried to comfort him, seeing the guilt spread across Lewis's face.

"See? It's okay. I'm fine," Taryn said.

Just then, the doctor walked into the room.

"Am I interrupting?" Dr. Matsura asked.

"No, not at all." Taryn sighed with a smile. "So what's the verdict, Doc?"

"Well, we had to put a total of five stitches in, so not too bad. And good news is, no concussion," Dr. Matsura replied.

"Phew! So I can sleep normal tonight!" Taryn exclaimed excitedly.

"Don't get ahead of yourself. Just for tonight, it would be smart to get some rest sitting up. Prop yourself up with some pillows and have someone monitor you. You'll have to see your regular physician in about two weeks to remove the stitches. Take it easy until then so they don't burst open, okay? Other than that, you should be good to go. My nurse will be in here soon with discharge papers and some medication to help with the pain. If anything changes, please come back here immediately," Dr. Matsura added.

"See! I told you I'm fine. It was probably the angle of the cut that made it bleed so much. Head tissue is very sensitive. But I knew I didn't have a concussion. I wasn't experiencing the symptoms, and I didn't even hit my head that hard. All you guys panicked for nothing," Taryn joked, rolling her eyes.

"It could have been way worse." Lewis sighed.

"Well, it wasn't. So get the fuck over it, okay? I'm already over it, and I'm thinking of what to watch when I get home since I gotta stay sitting up for most of the night." Taryn smiled.

"You're not going home," Lewis replied. "Doc said someone has to monitor you. Since I'm staying at my dad's tonight, you're going to stay with me like old times, okay? That way, we can take Jazzy home too."

"I don't think it can be like old times," Taryn said with a wink. "Doc said I have to take it easy remember?"

"Ti, you know what I meant," Lewis said in a serious tone.

"I know." She sighed. "But you're all down, and I don't like it."

"I'll go tell Tyson I'm catching a ride with you guys home. He figured you were going to drive Taryn home and stay there, but if you're staying at your dad's, I'll jump in with you guys," Jazzy said, exiting the room.

"Why don't you come and stay at my house again?" Taryn said. "If you still got that full-size bed, we both won't fit anymore now that you're all yoked out."

"Stop." Lewis sighed. "I told my dad and Mal I would stay there tonight so I can have breakfast with them in the morning. Dad was going to drop me off to the airport around lunchtime."

"Well, since you're watching me tonight, I can drop you off to the airport. I gotta pick up my parents at one anyways," Taryn replied.

"No deal," Lewis said.

"Yes deal, or I'm going to drive myself home after you fall asleep," Taryn argued.

"You're impossible sometimes, you know," Lewis retorted, getting frustrated with her stubbornness.

"I know, but you still love me for it. I keep things interesting that way." Taryn winked.

"Only sometimes though." Lewis smiled as he leaned down and gave Taryn a kiss on the forehead. Relief finally washed over his face, knowing that she was okay.

17

Nathan

Tiana and Noah were flying home tomorrow, so Sienna cooked a huge meal for them on their last night in the bay. They had been out shopping at Japantown, Trader Joe's, and the Korean market all day, getting omiyage to bring back home. By the end of it all, Nathan was exhausted. It was half past 2:00 a.m. when Nathan's phone went off with a text message from Taryn.

"Don't panic, but I'm at the ER. I fell down and hit my head. Thought I'd let you know before Jazzy ratted me out. Shhh! Don't tell Mom and Dad. Love you!" (Taryn)

Nathan was still half asleep reading it and thought he was dreaming. He sat up, turned on the bedside lamp, and rubbed his eyes, rereading the text again. It wasn't a dream, and he didn't misread it the first time. Something happened to Taryn...again. First, she went missing, and now she's at the ER? What the fuck was happening? He sat up in bed and called Taryn.

"Damnit it!" he said to himself as her call went straight to voicemail.

"What's going on?" Sienna asked, waking up.

"Taryn's in the emergency room." Nathan sighed with frustration.

"What? Is she okay?" Sienna asked, worried, fully awake now, and sitting up next to him.

"I don't know. She's not answering her phone. I think it might be dead because it's going straight to voicemail," Nathan said, trying Taryn again.

"Is there anyone else you could call?" Sienna suggested. "Maybe Jazzy?"

"I'll try her now," he replied, dialing Jazzy's number.

"Hello?" Jazzy's voice came over the line with a deep exhale.

"Jaz, are you with Taryn?" Nathan asked. "Do you know why she's in the ER?"

Nathan could hear his older cousin take a deep inhale of a cigarette before exhaling to answer.

"Yes, I'm with her. And yes, I know why," Jazzy replied. "Ti being Ti, she tried to break up a fight. Lewis was gonna pummel one of his boys for getting handsy with her. Something about his boy pinning her and forcing her to kiss him or something. Lewis was ready to kill him."

"So what happened?" Nathan asked, putting Jazzy on speaker so that Sienna could listen in.

"After Lewis checked to make sure Ti was okay, he went to charge at his boy. Ti stepped in between them to try and stop Lewis right as he started swinging. Ti caught the full force of his fist to her face, and she fell and hit her head on the pavement," Jazzy explained.

"What the fuck? Is she okay?" Nathan was awake now.

"Yeah, she's fine. Needed some stitches. Her jaw is a bit bruised, and her lip is busted, but no concussion, and she got meds for the pain. She's fucking tough," Jazzy sighed as she took another hit of her cigarette.

"Are you guys still at the ER?" Nathan asked.

"Yep. They're just waiting for the nurse to bring the discharge papers, and we should be heading home. Lewis is going to monitor her tonight just to be on the safe side," Jazzy replied.

"What the fuck is Lewis's problem? First, he hits her, and then he wants to take care of her? What the fuck?" Nathan was pissed.

"Calm down. It was an accident. He blanked out and didn't even see Ti run in front of him. He feels like shit right now," Jazzy scolded.

"Fuck that. He better feel like shit. How could he hit her like that?" Nathan's fists began to clench, his knuckles turning white at the thought of someone hitting his sister.

"Don't be mad at Lewis. He was trying to defend Taryn. If anything, be pissed at his boy Paul for trying to make a move on her. Apparently, that dude forced his tongue down her throat and grabbed her in all the no-no places," Jazzy tried to reason.

"Fuck both of them," Nathan seethed.

"Nathan, I'm going to tell you this one more time. Calm the fuck down. It was just a shitshow tonight. We all know that, but the main thing is that Taryn is okay. Lewis feels like shit, and Paul is going to get his ass beat later for starting all of this," Jazzy said sternly.

"Whatever. You tell Taryn to call me after she charges her phone, please," Nathan said.

"Only if you calm down and stop pointing blaming fingers at people when this was an accident," Jazzy argued.

"Fine! Just have her call me," Nathan said, hanging up the phone.

Sitting there in the dim lamplight, Sienna grabbed Nathan's hand and started to rub some comfort into it.

"Jazzy is right. The main thing is that Taryn is okay. Just hold on to that," Sienna soothed.

"She's not okay if she's in the ER and needed stitches," he argued.

"But she's alive, she doesn't have a concussion, and they're letting her go home already," Sienna retorted gently. "It could have been a lot worse."

"I guess you're right." Nathan sighed heavily. "Lewis is a beast next to Taryn. I'm surprised she only stumbled back. A punch full force from him should have made her black out or snapped her in half."

"Well, Ti is fucking tough." Sienna sighed with a laugh.

"Yeah. She's like a man trapped in a woman's body sometimes when it comes to shit like this. Her pain tolerance level is off the charts. Fucking weirdo," he replied, thinking of his sister.

"Do you think you should tell Derek?" Sienna asked.

"Nah, I wouldn't want to worry him," Nathan replied.

"Let me rephrase that. I think you should tell Derek," Sienna clarified.

On a heavy sigh in agreement with Sienna, Nathan found Derek's number in his phone and dialed. Despite it being in the middle of the night, Derek answered.

"Hello?" His voice was full of sleep.

"D, it's Nate," Nathan replied.

"Hey, Nate, what's up? Is everything okay?" Derek replied, sounding half awake.

"Yes and no. I figured I'd let you know so you can reach out to her, but Ti is in the emergency room," Nathan said.

You could hear immediate shuffling on the other end of the phone as the news of Taryn got Derek's attention, pulling him wide awake.

"What happened? Why is she there? Is she okay? Who's with her? Is she being admitted?" Panic was clear in Derek's voice.

"Whoa! Slow down and breathe, bro." Nathan tried to sound casual and calm talking to Derek so he wouldn't freak out too badly. "She got punched in the face pretty good when she went out with some old friends. One of them was going to fight. Ti got in the middle to break it up and took the punch to the face instead. She fell and hit her head."

"What!" Derek's panic suddenly turned into anger. "Who hit her? Is she okay?"

"Remember that Ti is a tough ass bitch. She's probably been rocked just as hard, if not harder, when she was cheering or when she got into fights herself. This one was just a lucky punch that hit her in the right place, but she is okay. She needed some stitches, and her face looks a little busted up, but she doesn't have a concussion. They're discharging her to go home soon," Nathan explained.

"Who the fuck hit her?" Derek was the one who was pissed now.

"It was her so-called friend Lewis. Apparently, he was going after one of his friends who tried to force himself onto Taryn. She didn't want Lewis fighting, so she stepped in between them to stop him, but it was too late. His fist was already coming down full force. It was an accident," Nathan said sarcastically.

"I thought this Lewis guy was there to take care of her? He's hitting her instead? What the fuck?" Derek's voice was erratic.

"That's what I said. But our cousin Jazzy insisted it was an accident and that Lewis was only doing that to protect Taryn. It was her fault for getting in the way anyways, knowing Lewis's temper. Back in the day, his temper usually had him blacking out if he was that mad. With his size now and how many fights he's gotten into in the past, he would've destroyed whichever friend he was going after. Ti stepped in to save him from himself, I guess," Nathan continued.

"Thanks for letting me know, Nate. I'll try calling her now. She hasn't responded to my text that I sent her earlier. She left me on unread," Derek said, exasperated.

"No problem. Her phone might be dead though. I tried calling too, and it went straight to voicemail," Nathan replied.

"I'll still try. Thanks, Nate. Night," Derek said, hanging up.

Nathan couldn't believe what was going on. First the flying home, then the Toby drama, her disappearing, and now Taryn was in the ER? It was too much to take. He was scared that little by little, his sister was being pushed further over the edge. How much more could she take before she fell over? He didn't know, and he could only hope that they wouldn't have to find out.

18

Derek

For the first time since the start of his career, he despised being an actor. In the past, when he'd have to film on three-day holiday weekends or occasionally miss a family gathering here and there, it wasn't a big deal to him. His family understood, and he knew when he became more successful, he'd be able to be there for them when he had more of a say in the roles he played.

But right now, hearing that Taryn was in the ER, he felt helpless. He wanted to run to her, to be by her side and make sure she was okay, but his contract restricted him to do so. Granted, it would be different if it were a family emergency and it was his parent or one of his sisters in the hospital, but wasn't it the same if he cared for Taryn just as much?

Taryn never responded to the text he sent earlier, and it was weighing heavily on his heart. At this point, he needed to talk to her, hear her voice, let her hear him say the words himself. Even if he knew it was late and she hadn't answered Nathan's calls, Derek had to try. After letting the line ring five times, he was just about ready to hang up when a female voice came over the line.

"Hello?" the voice said shortly.

"Um, hi. Is Taryn there?" Derek asked meekly, slightly relieved someone answered because it meant she didn't block his number like he initially believed.

"Yeah, but she's kinda out of it. I'm just charging her phone for her in the waiting room. She should be discharged soon though, so I'll let her know you called," the voice responded.

"Oh, okay. Thank you. This is Derek, by the way. Just tell her I hope she's okay, and I hope to hear from her soon, please," he replied.

"Wait a minute. So this is Derek, huh?" the voice questioned.

"Um, yes?" he responded, confused.

"The Derek from San Francisco, the one she met at her brother's graduation?" the female continued to ask.

"Yes," Derek replied, unsure of where this conversation was going.

"So you're the Derek that weaseled his way into my baby cousin's pants after one night, huh? Then you're suddenly confessing your love for her? When you don't even know her yet?" the voice barked over the phone.

Derek was stunned. He had no idea what to say or how to respond to that. This older cousin was clearly protective of Taryn and did not seem to like him at all.

"This is Jazzy, by the way. I'm like her older sister," Jazzy finally introduced herself to Derek with sass. "I'm not trying to scare you or grill you about fucking around with my baby cousin. She's grown, and she can make her own choices. But I will say this…she's been through a lot, so whatever this game is that you're playing with her, just don't. She's too good to be used and have her heart broken again, okay? It's not fair to her," Jazzy said seriously.

"I can promise you that I'm not using Taryn. Since I met her at the graduation, I've been drawn to her. The more time I spent with her, the more I think about her, the more I feel this need to just be around her. And even if I barely know her and still have a lot to learn, I know what I feel for her. It may even sound crazy, but when you know, you know," Derek defended.

"Well, everyone is drawn to her. That's why we're in the ER right now." Jazzy sighed, frustrated.

"Nathan called and told me what happened," Derek explained.

"He did? Usually it takes Nathan years to warm up to someone Taryn is talking to. He's always been silently protective that way.

That's kinda crazy that he's already on your side enough to give you Ti updates." Jazzy was shocked.

"Well, maybe because he's known me for a while? My little sister is one of his best friends from college, and now she's dating his roommate, Reggie. He didn't like the idea of me with his sister at first. Even threatened me to stay away from her," Derek reasoned.

"Sounds like Nate." Jazzy laughed. "Wait, is your sister Emma? She came down one spring break with all the boys and crashed at Taryn's house. I remember her. She's sweet."

"Yeah, that's my sister. She was the instigator in all of this initially, but after spending five minutes with Taryn, I couldn't help but crumble at her feet," Derek replied.

"That's Ti for you. Even when she does stupid shit and ends up in the ER, you can't help but want to cuddle her like she's a newborn puppy. She drives me crazy sometimes," Jazzy said.

"Well, I really do hope she's okay. She hasn't been responding to my texts or calls, and now hearing she's in the ER, and she won't even talk to me to let me know she's okay, it's driving me insane," Derek said, his voice drenched in worry.

"Wait, why isn't she talking to you?" Jazzy questioned.

"She's under the impression that I have something going on with my ex, but it was just a huge misunderstanding. Before I could even talk to her about it, she flew home to Hawai'i, and according to Nathan, it's been rough for her since she landed," Derek explained.

"You have no idea, but I'll definitely tell her to call you. You seem genuine enough. Just remember, you better not hurt her, or you'll have all of Hawai'i on your ass," Jazzy warned.

"I promise I won't. Thank you again. Good night," Derek said as he heard Jazzy hang up the phone on the other end of the line.

Sighing heavily to himself, he felt a little better. If Jazzy was as close to Taryn as she said she was, maybe she could be the buffer that would get Taryn to talk to him again. Hearing from someone who was with Taryn also eased his nerves a little, knowing that she was in fact all right. He was just anxious to talk to her himself now. On a heavy sigh, he closed his eyes and thought of her face as exhaustion took over.

19

Lewis

Lewis pulled the car into his dad's driveway and Jazzy got out of the backseat, gathering all of Taryn's belongings. Lewis, walking over to the passenger door, opened it and lifted Taryn, cradling her gently in his arms, being careful as to not hit her head on anything.

"Lewis, I can walk," Taryn said sarcastically, trying to fidget so he would put her down.

Without responding, Lewis just pulled her even tighter into his chest until she relaxed in his arms. Using Lewis's keys, Jazzy unlocked the front door and followed Lewis into the house. His room was at the rear of the house, closest to the back door, and was the only one on the main floor. Lewis was always grateful for this because it allowed him to come and go as he pleased when he was younger without worrying about waking his dad. The same went for tonight. He was not prepared to explain to his dad what happened to Taryn when he was supposed to be the one protecting her.

"Just put her stuff on my dresser over there," Lewis told Jazzy as he pointed to a black dresser in the corner of his room. "Thanks for all of your help, Jazzy."

"No problem. She's my little sis. Just call me if you need anything, or if she gets worse," Jazzy said.

"I will," Lewis replied as he gently placed Taryn down onto the softness of his comforter.

"Ti, let him take care of you, okay? I'll see you in the morning," Jazzy said to Taryn, giving her knee a little squeeze before turning to leave.

Seeing Taryn in his bed again brought back countless memories of their year together. Some nights they would lay there, just watching television or talking about new authors they were reading. He could never talk with his boys about stuff like that, or he'd never hear the end of it. Other nights, they got lost in each other, filling every inch of his room with pleasure as he buried himself deep inside of her for hours. Either way, nights with her next to him, in that very bed, gave him some of the best memories in his life. He stared down at her, and his heart couldn't help but ache thinking about it.

"Ti, you can lay back on my pillows. It's okay. I can wash them tomorrow," Lewis said, knowing she was self-conscious about getting whatever blood the doctors didn't clean off her onto his bedding.

"I feel really gross though. I want to actually wash my hair, not that half-dry rubdown crap they did at the hospital," Taryn said, tilting her head, trying to see how much of her hair was still matted in her blood.

"You can't. Doctor said not to wet your stitches for at least twenty-four hours," Lewis argued.

"This is so gross though," Taryn whined, unable to get past leaving the blood in her hair.

"Can we compromise then?" Lewis asked. "I'll draw you a bath and I'll clean around your stitches as best I can with warm water and soap. But you can't do it yourself because I know you, and I know you're going to end up scrubbing your entire head like normal with the shampoo."

Taryn sat there for a while, contemplating her options. He knew she was tired but wouldn't sleep or relax until she got to shower. She always had this thing about not being able to go to bed unless she felt clean. Even if they showered before going out, she would always rinse off or at least wash her feet before laying down in bed. And if she was sweating or got dirty at all, she would have to take a full shower before she could relax. He waited in anticipation for her answer, seeing the frustration form on her brow.

"Fine," she said, rolling her eyes on a heavy sigh.

He smiled to himself, knowing how much she would hate this and pout. Taryn was always so independent. The thought of someone caring for her, to the extent of bathing her, was probably killing her inside right now. He laughed to himself as she got up and stalked off to the bathroom.

Lewis filled the guest bathtub downstairs with hot water, the steam fogging the mirror and making the air thick. Still hurting from her fall, Taryn gingerly began trying to pull her tank top off over her head. A sudden sharp inhale of air from Taryn caught Lewis's attention immediately. He turned off the faucet of the tub and rushed over to her to help.

"Lewis, I got it," Taryn said meekly.

"Stop, it's fine. Let me help before you hurt yourself more," Lewis argued.

"I'm just a little sore. I guess we were all so worried about my head busting open that I didn't even realize my body hit the ground pretty hard." Taryn giggled. "I think these body aches are worse than the throbbing of my head right now."

"Why are you laughing? It's not funny. You're hurt," Lewis said, concerned.

"If I don't laugh, I'll end up crying, that's why," Taryn said honestly as Lewis maneuvered the last of the material over her head, avoiding her stitches.

"It's okay to cry in front of me," Lewis said, kissing Taryn on the forehead as he pushed her hair from her eyes.

"Not over something as silly as a little accident. The other stuff, hell yes. I'll soak your chest in my snot all day. But not over something like this, especially when I'm okay," Taryn said with a smile.

"You don't have to be tough all the time" Lewis retorted as he used his body to brace Taryn up as she slipped out of her leggings.

"True, but that's just me. You know that, Lewis. I'm not one to cry for reason or over stupid stuff. I get mad at myself when I do," she said, scoffing.

She took a step back to stretch the tension from her muscles. Lewis took in the sight of her as her bra dropped to the ground. Even after all these years, her petite frame was still tight and toned. The only difference is the obvious plumpness in her chest and behind, her body filling out in all the right places now that she wasn't burning fat at cheer practice twenty hours a week. Feeling the blood in his body rushing downward, he tried to steady his breath as he realized suddenly, that she was naked standing before him. In a feeble attempt to avert his eyes from staring, he turned to face the corner.

"Just let me know when you're in the tub so I can start rinsing your hair out," Lewis said, his voice cracking.

"You're being silly now." Taryn laughed. "It's nothing you haven't seen, Lewis. Even before we were fooling around, you saw me naked. Remember those times when I was a lightweight drinking, threw up on myself, and you had to strip me down and shower me? It's not a big deal."

"Well, as your student now, it's not appropriate, Professor," Lewis said jokingly.

"Oh my gosh." Taryn chuckled, shaking her head. "Whatever. I'm in the tub."

He turned slowly. Taryn was sunken down into the water, the soap suds hiding her body from him but not giving him any added comfort knowing that her familiar deliciousness was hiding just beneath the surface. Every time she took a breath in, he could see her breasts move the bubbles. Trying to focus on taking care of her, Lewis knelt down next to the tub. He filled a little cup with tub water and began wetting her hair, slowly working his way up toward where the gash lay.

"Ow!" Taryn flinched.

"What?" Lewis dropped the cup, and his hands shot up into the air, his eyes searching her head for where he might have hurt her or touched her stitches.

"Just kidding," Taryn said, laughing as she turned to him.

"That's not funny," Lewis said, his heart threatening to jump from his chest.

"It is when you look like that now," Taryn said, lifting a hand and wiping soap bubbles from Lewis's face. His reaction had sent a plethora of suds from the tub up into the air and all over him.

"Thanks. I needed a wash too," Lewis said sarcastically.

"You were kneeling on the nasty parking lot ground and stayed with me in the germ-filled ER. You definitely need a shower too," Taryn retorted with sass. Lewis shook his head as he washed the blood from Taryn's hair.

"Lew?" Taryn said suddenly, her tone serious.

"Yeah?" he replied.

"Thank you," Taryn said sweetly. "I don't think anyone could truly understand our friendship, but I know that I appreciate it. I'm sorry for taking it for granted before."

"Well, I'm sorry for punching you. I guess we could call it even now," Lewis joked.

As he finished lathering and rinsing her hair, being careful as to avoid her stitches, he instinctively reached down between her legs to drain the water. His fingers brushed accidentally on the soft flesh of her inner thigh, her breath catching ever so slightly.

"Sorry," he said, looking down, freezing with his hand on the drain plug.

"Don't be." Taryn smiled trying to calm her breathing.

He leaned back on his knees, and his arm hovered at the edge of the tub as he stared at her. Even in her disheveled state, with the cut on her bottom lip, she was still beautiful.

"What?" Taryn asked nervously. "Am I bleeding somewhere else?" She started to feel around her face and neck for another cut.

"No." He sighed with a smile. "I just missed you, that's all. Didn't realize how much until just now."

"I missed you too," Taryn said, smiling back at him.

"Come on. Let's get you out of there before you get all pruned," Lewis said, standing and holding out a towel for her.

Taryn got up slowly and stepped out, letting Lewis wrap her up in the towel. Gently, he picked her up and carried her back to his room, setting her down on the edge of his bed.

"So..." Taryn started with a heavy inhale.

"You need to borrow clothes again?" Lewis said, laughing.

"Yes, please," she said with an innocent smile.

"Help yourself to my closet," Lewis replied as he turned to go clean up the bathroom and take a quick shower himself.

Glancing back over his shoulder before closing his bedroom door, he couldn't help but smile. It was truly like old times all over again.

20

Taryn

Taryn knew who her true friends were when it came to times like this. Even after years of not talking, she could still rely on them to pick up as if no time had passed at all, and they would have each other's back. That was the kind of friend Lewis was to her. Despite the slight awkwardness, and ten years of sexual tension built up from fooling around before, when it came down to it, Lewis made caring for her his priority. As she stood in his towel and began shuffling through his closet, she pulled down a plain black T-shirt and threw it on. She bunched it in the front and took a deep inhale. It still smelled like Lewis, even if he probably hadn't worn it since he moved to California.

Turning to his drawers, she pulled open the second drawer to the bottom and yanked out a pair of gray sweatpants when a worn white envelope floated to the ground. Picking up the envelope and turning it over, she found her name written on the front in Lewis's handwriting.

"What the fuck?" Taryn said aloud to herself, confused, as she turned the envelope in her hand. Why would Lewis have something like this but not give it to her? How old was this? Was he trying to hide this from her?

Curious as to why she was seeing this for the first time, she opened the envelope to find a handwritten letter, addressed to her from Lewis. It read:

My dearest Taryn,

Let me start by saying how happy I am for you. For the first time in your life, since the first time I saw you from over the fence at your uncle's house, you seem truly content. You're always working so hard and taking care of everyone else. It's about time someone took care of you. And I hope he does. I see your posts on social media, and it is bittersweet for me to see you so happy yet no longer seeming to need me in your life.

But if I'm being honest with myself, I'm not happy at all. If anything, it breaks my heart a little more each time I see you with him. Knowing he's holding your hand instead of me. Knowing you're falling asleep in his arms instead of mine. It's killing me a little at a time, and I can't take it anymore. I'm sorry. I never wanted to be that guy, but if I can't be with you, I don't know if we can be just friends. It hurts too much to know how my heart yearns for you knowing I can never tell you how I truly feel. Knowing I lost my chance.

It's not your fault though. It's mine. I keep telling myself, maybe if I had the balls to just tell you how I felt, you and I would be together. But I was too late. It's true, you know. You never know what you truly have until it's gone. I'm sorry for taking what we had for granted and thinking it would last forever that way without making an effort to tell you how I felt about you.

I wish you knew how much I love you, as more than just a friend. Sometimes I feel as if I love you more than life itself. I wanted to honor and cherish you all the days of my life, but I could never bring myself to speak those words to your face, and maybe that's why I lost you. I think we would've been really amazing together, not just because this was the best year of my life but because our relationship would have been founded on such a strong friendship first.

I've never had someone like you in my life, Taryn. You lift me up, encourage me, support me, make me want to be a better person and do better for myself. I'm just sorry I realized all of this too late. Now you're with him, and I want you to be happy, so I'll keep all of this to myself. But if I could tell you how I felt, if I got one more shot to make you my girl, I would tell you how much I love you, how my life has become so empty and lost without you in it. How, if I had you as mine, I would never let you go.

I know it's too late though, and that's on me for fucking up. I'm sorry. I do wish you the best, and I hope he loves and cares for you as much as I do because if he doesn't, I'll be waiting for the day to be good enough for you.

Yours now and always,
Lewis

Taryn couldn't believe what she just read. Their friends, even Jazzy and his sister Mal, would joke about them being the perfect couple. Tyson and Kyle were forever instigating trying to get them to date, but what they had just worked. Never in a million years did Taryn imagine Lewis would actually have these kinds of feelings for her. He was your ultimate bachelor, and girls drooled over him every chance they got. Taryn just saw herself as the dorky neighbor that grew up with him. She was not like any of the girls Lewis had dated before either. If anything, she felt like she wasn't good enough for him.

That year, they were messing around, that's all she thought it was. That they were just friends with benefits since they were both single and at least knew that the other was "clean" down there. At one point, Taryn did have feelings for Lewis, but she never acted on them or pushed it because she knew Lewis wasn't a commitment type of guy. She figured if he saw her as anything more than a friend that he would tell her, but he never did. So, she accepted their situation as is.

With the towel wrapped around her waist, sweatpants in one hand and the letter in the other, she sat on the edge of Lewis's bed in shock. She reread the letter over and over again as she tried to comprehend what she just found out. When did he write this letter? It couldn't have been recently because the edges of the paper were browning and thinning as if it were really old. Was this from when he found out she was dating Toby? Why didn't he give her the letter? A thousand questions ran through her mind, giving her a headache.

"You found clothes?" Lewis asked as he came back into the room, closing the door behind him.

"What is this?" Taryn said, on the verge of crying from being overwhelmed as she held the letter up to Lewis.

His eyes suddenly widened as he stopped breathing altogether, the blood draining from his face. He froze in front of her like a deer in the headlights.

"Lewis, what is this?" Taryn asked again, her voice shaking. "You said you had feelings, but you were in legit, love-love with me?"

"Where did you find that?" he stuttered, panicked.

"In your drawer. It fell out when I grabbed some sweatpants," Taryn explained.

"I thought you were grabbing basketball shorts?" Lewis asked.

"I was cold, so I went for some sweatpants. How was I supposed to know you were hiding this from me in that drawer?" Taryn said angrily.

"I, um, I…" Lewis hesitated, trying to find the right words.

Frustrated, Taryn slapped the letter into his chest as she ripped the towel off her waist, exposing herself to him. Without hesitation, she yanked on the sweatpants with a scoff, and she stormed back to his dresser, grabbing her things.

"Where are you going?" Lewis suddenly snapped out of it.

"Home," Taryn said harshly.

"No, you're not. You can't drive right now. It's late, you haven't slept yet, and you need someone to monitor you overnight, the doctor said," Lewis argued.

"Yes, I am. I'd rather take my chances sleeping alone than being here with someone who hid such a huge secret from me for so long!" Taryn seethed.

Lewis stepped back from her for a second, her words clearly hurting him. Suddenly, he shot his body in between her and the door, blocking her exit.

"No, you're not," Lewis reiterated. "Please, just let me explain."

"No! I'm tired of everyone trying to tell me what's best for me or explain shit they think I don't know," Taryn spat at him. "No one can explain to me how I feel! It's either people keep telling me what I should do, or they don't tell me at all because they think they'll mess me up. I'm so sick of it! Maybe if I knew the whole truth, I could at least make decisions for myself! So please, get out of my way!"

"Ti, I don't know who is trying to tell you how to feel or explain what they think you should feel, but it's me. It's Lewis. You know me better than anyone. Please stop for a second and hear me out," Lewis pleaded.

"Oh yeah? I know you?" Taryn scoffed. "That letter sure doesn't support that idea. If we knew each other so well, you would've known how much I yearned to just hear those words from you ten fucking years ago."

Using all the strength in her, Taryn pushed past Lewis and yanked at the door, but it wouldn't budge. Lewis had turned around and was towering over her from behind, using the full weight of his body to keep the door shut and prevent her from leaving.

"Taryn, please," he said, his voice cracking as he rested his lips on the back of her head. "Don't leave."

"My stitches," she said, hoping to scare him off her enough for her to yank the door open.

"I'm nowhere near your stitches," he said with confidence as he remained solidly in place. "Please, Taryn, just give me ten minutes."

They stood there in silence for a while, neither willing to budge. Taryn's breath was heavy, anger and pain radiating from her body. Lewis didn't know what to do to calm her down. Slowly, he snaked his arms down the door and around her waist, pulling her to him from behind as he leaned down to rest his chin on her shoulder.

"Please, Ti, for old times' sake," he whispered into her ear as he kissed her on the cheek. He could feel the tension in her body start to subside, her heartbeat increasing. "Stay with me, please."

"No. I can't do this right now, Lewis." Taryn started to shake as tears welled in her eyes.

"Ti, please. Don't go. I'm sorry. Just please, please let me explain." Lewis's voice cracked as he squeezed her harder. She could feel his tears on her shoulder, wetting the material of his shirt.

"I'll let you know when I get home." Taryn shrugged him off, and before he knew it, she was out the door.

She refused to glance over her shoulder, afraid she might crumble and turn around if she saw his face. Taryn rushed to her car, started the engine, and peeled off as Lewis's figure appeared in the street in her rearview mirror.

There was everything with Toby, the old wounds he had ripped anew. Then, there was the mess to deal with back in San Francisco with Derek, whom she was still unsure what his text earlier was all about. Now, having to deal with this letter from Lewis on top of it all, basically confessing he felt the same for her all those years ago and neither of them had the courage to express their feelings to one another, it was just too much. Taryn was being pushed to her breaking point. But then again, what did she expect? Going from how they were together that year to no contact whatsoever over the last ten? Now she suddenly expected everything to be normal between them? As if nothing happened? It was too good to be true, and Taryn knew it. Deep inside, she knew she loved Lewis, but she wasn't sure in what way, and his letter confused her even more now. She had to figure out what she was feeling soon because she refused to cause pain to those she cared about, especially if it were anything like the pain she felt from Toby.

21

Nathan

Nathan and Sienna had just dropped Tiana and Noah off to the airport and were headed back into the city to the apartment. Nathan didn't tell his parents anything about Taryn's eventful night in the ER. He figured she could tell them when she picked them up from the airport. He just wished he could be there to see what excuse she came up with to explain her busted face and stitches in her head. Using the car's Bluetooth, he dialed Taryn to let her know Tiana and Noah were at the airport already.

"Hello?" Taryn said sleepily.

It was 8:00 a.m. in San Francisco, but the two-hour time difference meant it was barely 6:00 a.m. in Hawai'i. More than likely, Taryn had just gotten home from the ER and fallen asleep.

"WAKE UP!" Nathan yelled.

"What the fuck! You're so loud. Can you not?" Taryn retorted.

"I'll stop talking loud if you start talking. What the fuck happened last night? How's your head?" Nathan asked.

"Hold on a sec," Taryn replied. "I just sent you the pics from the ER. The first one is before the stitches, the second is after, and the third is my face. My lip is just a little busted, and I got a small bruise under my eye. I'm okay though."

Sienna opened the messages on Nathan's phone, revealing Taryn's injuries. She gasped at the photo of the gash in Taryn's head before holding his phone in front of the dashboard for him to see.

"Damn, Ti! Are you okay? It looks so bad!" Sienna said.

"Yeah. I'm good. My head hurts a little, but it looks worse than it feels, promise," Taryn replied.

"So what the fuck happened? I heard Lewis hit you?" Nathan said, trying to keep his cool as he gripped the wheel.

"It was an accident. When we were saying our goodbyes in the parking lot, his friend Paul tried to grope me. He yanked me to him, wouldn't let me go, then shoved his tongue down my throat." Taryn shuddered, reliving the memory. "Lewis yanked him off me, made sure I was okay, and was going to kill him."

"So why'd you get in the middle?" Nathan asked.

"Lewis's in the military now. He can't just fight like he used to, or he'd get into big trouble. So I stepped in between them and was going to try to push him back, but his fist was already swinging down at Paul. It all happened so fast. Next thing I know, Lewis is a blubbering mess of guilt and I'm on the ground holding my face." Taryn sighed.

"So he was trying to protect you? Didn't he see you, though, when you got in front of him?" Nathan questioned.

"Nate, he's like you. When he gets to that point of being pissed, he blanks. He only snapped out of it because he heard me sobbing like a little bitch," Taryn reasoned.

"If I got punched in the face by a guy as big as Lewis, I would be on the ground sobbing too," Nathan said sarcastically. "Still pissed he hit you though. Protecting you or not, he should have been more aware of himself, especially since he's in the military, and they get trained on shit like that, right? Plus, imagine if that was his kid and he blanked. He gotta be careful with that shit."

"I agree, and I talked to him about it. But bottom line, it was an accident. It was no one's fault, and bottom line number 2, I'm okay," Taryn replied.

"All right, well, I'm glad you're okay, dumbass. I don't know why you tried to stop him in the first place. If he's bigger than he was when we were growing up, he's probably a monster now," Nathan said.

"Yeah, kinda. I guess I'm not as invincible as I thought I was, huh?" Taryn sighed.

"No, you're not. And with that being said, avoiding hard conversations with people or running away doesn't make you invincible to being hurt," Nathan argued.

"What are you talking about? I'm not afraid of being hurt, and I haven't avoided any conversations with anyone," Taryn retorted.

"Derek." Nathan said his name, causing Taryn to sigh heavily on the other end of the line. "Talk to him. He's been a mess, Ti. It was a huge misunderstanding, and he's been constantly wanting to hang with us to feel close to you. I'm not a college boy anymore, you know? This going out to keep him company all the time is tiring," he joked.

"Derek?" Taryn questioned. "You've been hanging out with Derek since I left?"

"Yes, Ti," Nathan said. "I don't know what you did to that poor kid, but he is mush over you."

Over the past few days, Nathan truly began to feel for Derek. He was going to give Derek a chance this summer because he was Emma's brother, but after getting to know him better and hearing how sincere he was about his feelings for Taryn, Nathan truly started to like the dude. He felt bad that Taryn misinterpreted and made assumptions about Derek's kiss with his ex. If Taryn let him explain himself, it would all work out, and she might have a shot at finding happiness again, and that's all Nathan ever wanted for her.

"I'll text him." Taryn sighed.

"Okay," Nathan responded. "Whatever you do, please be up front with him. Don't give him hope if there's no way in hell you'd give it a shot with him this summer. Don't be that type of girl, okay? Because that's not the Ti that I know."

Nathan had to slip that last little note in. Before he met Sienna, he had been in Derek's shoes before. He truly fell head over heels for this girl from San Jose state, but she had led him on and gave him glimmers of hope that they could be together, but he ultimately wasted six months of his life chasing something that was never going to happen.

"Yes, Dad," Taryn teased.

"All right, get some rest and I'll call you when I hear that Mom and Dad landed," Nathan replied.

"Thanks, Nate," she replied.

"Of course. I got you, as long as you don't go getting yourself punched in the face again," he joked.

He could hear his sister sigh as she hung up the phone. Man, would they have an interesting summer to look forward to.

22

Lewis

Lewis knew he couldn't chase her. When Taryn got into these moods, she just needed time and space to calm down before you could talk to her. Trying to push it would just push her away even further. It didn't make her being upset with him and leaving like that hurt or make him worry any less. She would have to talk to him eventually; he was taking one of her courses this summer. Hopefully, they'd be able to talk before then, because he didn't know if he could sit through classes and give her his attention without having the urge to yell out and explain himself to her.

"Morning, boy!" Lewis's dad, George, said as he slapped his son firmly on the back, making him sit up at the dining room table. "Rough night? You didn't even make it into your room."

"Kind of. I'm all right though," Lewis replied nonchalantly.

"Saw Taryn storm off last night," George responded.

Lewis straightened his back, stunned at his dad's revelation. He saw them? Did he know what happened?

"Security cameras," George explained, pointing through the living room window to the camera mounted on the garage wall outside. "Got 'em about six months back."

"Oh." Lewis sighed. "Yeah, she was here last night."

"Why didn't she stay?" George asked. "She could've."

Clearly George didn't hear their little argument last night, and it brought little relief to Lewis's mind.

"It was just a little awkward," Lewis tried to explain without details.

"Look, son, you don't gotta talk to me about it if you don't want to. I remember you going through it when you two were...whatever you were. But know I'm here. That's what family is for, okay? No judgments," George said, sitting down and resting a hand on Lewis's shoulder. "Just no tears. Rivera men don't cry," he added jokingly.

Lewis hung his head on a heavy sigh. His dad was right. He had to talk to someone about it, but he didn't know where to even start.

"Taryn ended up in the ER last night because I hit her," Lewis said softly.

"You what?" George questioned, thinking he confusingly heard what his son said.

"You hit Ti?" Mal's voice echoed in the front doorway.

"Mal, what are you doing here?" Lewis asked.

"I came to have breakfast with you guys before you left to go back to California again, duh." She scoffed. "Now what happened with Ti?"

Lewis sighed heavily, got up, and walked over to the kitchen counter, gripping it for stability and to face the impending wrath he'd soon suffer from his family for not only hitting a girl but hitting Taryn specifically.

"I already feel like shit, so please just hear me out first before you guys make me feel any worse about myself, okay?" Lewis pleaded.

George and Mal remained quiet, their eyes firmly focused on Lewis, silently urging him to continue. So Lewis recapped the night for them. He told them about what happened with Paul, who initiated it, how he went for blood, how Taryn tried to stop him so he wouldn't get in trouble. After explaining to his dad and sister how Taryn ended up in the emergency room, he sat down with a heavy sigh.

"I feel like shit for it," Lewis admitted.

"Bro, it's not your fault. Ti was stupid for trying to stop you. She's like the size of your forearm. What was she expecting to happen?" Mal reasoned.

"Son, it sincerely sounds like an accident, and we all know how much you care about Taryn. You would never intentionally hurt her like that," George added.

"If it was an accident, then why do I feel so crappy?" Lewis asked.

"Because you care about her. And because you care about her, it hurts you to see her hurt," Mal explained.

"Huh?" Lewis asked, confused. "What does that even mean?"

"You idiot." She laughed. "You care about Ti so much, you just don't want to see her hurt, and the fact that you hurt her, even on accident, makes you mad at yourself for being the cause of her pain."

"Exactly!" George said. "It's okay to fuck up. Ti knows you would never intentionally hurt her, that's why. And she cares enough about you to forgive you and see last night for what it was—just an accident. Don't beat yourself up about it. Is that why she left? You kept blaming yourself?"

"Yes and no." Lewis sighed nervously. "She had to go pick up her parents from the airport. That's why she went home to switch cars so she could just throw their suitcases in the back of her dad's truck."

"Oh…okay. See? Everything is good then, boy! Keep your head up." George smiled, standing from the table to start cooking.

"Will do, Dad," Lewis said, sighing and heading back to his room to clear his mind a bit before breakfast.

"So why did Taryn really leave last night?" Mal asked, popping into his room and shutting the door behind her.

"Huh?" Lewis asked.

"I know you, Lew. If she hit her head the way she did, there's no way in hell you would've just let her go home by herself, driving that late. You care too much. If that was the case, you would've gone home with her and drove with her back here in the morning for breakfast. So what happened here after the ER that you're not telling Dad?" Mallory said, dead on.

"Fuck." Lewis sighed, getting up and pulling the letter from his drawer, handing it to her.

Taking the pieces of paper and sitting cross-legged on his bed, Mal began to read in silence. The tension was heavy in the air as he did not know how his sister would react.

"Wow." She sighed finally. "I never knew you legit felt-felt stuff for her."

"I didn't know, too, until I saw her with Toby," he replied, taking the letter and shoving it back into his drawer.

"So I'm guessing she found the letter and things got awkward?" Mal questioned.

"Kinda. She was more pissed than anything else," Lewis explained.

"What do you mean she was pissed?" his sister said, confused.

"Like she was mad-mad. She kept questioning why I never gave the letter to her or why didn't I just tell her how I felt. Then she went on ranting about how everyone tries to explain to her how she's supposed to feel and how sick she is of not being able to make decisions because she doesn't know the whole truth," Lewis recalled. "I had no idea what to do or say. I never saw her so emotionally frustrated before. My mind could barely keep up with what she was saying. Even with the Toby mess, she kept her composure."

"You don't get it, do you?" His sister scoffed.

"No, I don't! I literally just said I didn't understand half of the crap she was yelling at me for," Lewis argued.

"She was in love with you. The only reason she probably ended up dating Toby was because your dumb ass didn't have the balls to tell her you felt the same way. After a year of fucking around and her waiting for you to grow some, she moved on," Mal explained.

"If she wanted to know how I felt, how come she didn't just ask me?" Lewis replied.

"One, if she asked you, would you have told her how you felt? How you really felt? And two, we all know your reputation as being a player, Lew. You weren't one to commit to anyone, *ever*. So of course, she didn't expect you to feel the same way," she seethed.

"I don't get why she's mad though." Lewis sighed.

"Being a female? I can tell you why, you idiot!" Mal continued. "Ti is probably beating herself up right now, that's why. Thinking that if she had just waited a little while longer, she could have had a chance to be with one of her best friends. Or maybe if she was more patient, she wouldn't have wasted how many years of her life with someone who just ended up cheating on her and leaving her anyways. Maybe if she had been with you instead, her life would be different."

Lewis fell silent, taking everything into consideration.

"Also as a female, just pointing this out, Taryn wouldn't have stuck around for a player type for a whole year if she didn't care about you, so don't even try to use the argument that you didn't know how she felt too," Mallory continued. "Ti has more respect for herself than that, and she wouldn't have let herself be used as your booty call if she didn't have feelings for you Lewis. Think about it."

She turned to leave him with his thoughts, getting up from his bed and closed his door behind her. Lewis began getting more frustrated with himself. Had his mistake in not telling Taryn how he felt ruined both of their lives? How different would their lives be if he just told her how he felt? He always thought she was too good for him, but was that just this excuse to not be honest with her? As he packed his bags, the smell of eggs and bacon filled his room, and he smiled thinking how lucky he was to be able to have Taryn in the Bay Area with him this summer. Maybe he could fix things, and they could finally see the true heights their friendship could take them to.

23

Taryn

Unable to fall back asleep, Taryn opened up her laptop and started a new project in Garage Band. Grabbing her mom's old guitar, she began playing chords over and over again, trying to soothe herself. Slowly, she began to pick the keys she created for the Mother's Day poem she turned into a song for Trish.

"Just get through doing this and you can close that chapter of your life." She sighed. "One step at a time."

As she began stroking the strings on the guitar, the song began to flow from her, the emotions within her building. Looking at the lyrics she had typed out on another window of her computer screen, she began to sing quietly, her words drenched with feelings.

> *Life may take control, time may pull us apart*
> *Your love'll always be there, wherever we may go*
> *Life's a long test, we'll question our hearts*
> *We learn from mistakes, time'll help us grow*

After playing the song in its entirety for the first time in what seemed like forever, Taryn lost herself in the music. The words flowed from her, and the strumming of the guitar came as natural as breathing. She hit record on her computer and left all her emotions on the track. Regardless of how she was feeling, she gave herself to the song and let the words absorb everything she had been through, tears pouring down her eyes as she sang.

> *Through every win, every fall*
> *You've kept me standing tall*
> *You're my light through it all*

After finishing the song, she exported the recording and sent it to Toby, closing that door once and for all in her life. It was in this moment that Taryn realized she was hurting inside more than she could have ever imagined. She truly felt broken beyond repair, and the more she tried to move on, the more it seemed as if she was messing things up, hurting more people. How could she be there for those she loved or set a positive example for her students if she barely knew who she was herself anymore?

Opening up a new document on her computer, she began to write. As an English teacher, she always taught her students that writing was her favorite subject because it was an amazing way to heal. Writing didn't have to be to anyone or for anyone or with a specific purpose at all. Writing was a way to vent privately, and in this moment, Taryn just needed to write everything down as a way to get it off her chest already. She was finally going to face herself so she could take a step toward facing her future.

24

Derek

The clock in his trailer read about a quarter past ten. Derek had not been able to sleep since Nathan told him that Taryn was in the emergency room. He had called her and left her messages, but she hadn't even read anything since he texted her that he loved her. It was disheartening to him, and it made it difficult for him to think of anything else.

"Hey, D, director said we're going to shoot the classroom scenes in twenty. You ready?" Ananya said, popping her head into his trailer.

"Yeah, I'll be right out." Derek sighed.

"You okay?" she asked, inviting herself in. "You were on point with the first couple of scenes we shot today, but you seemed out of it whenever we weren't rolling."

"Sorry," he said, hanging his head. "I didn't get much sleep last night."

"So you and Taryn good? You spent the night making up?" Ananya joked with a wink.

"No, she's still in Hawai'i." He laughed half-heartedly.

"That doesn't mean you guys couldn't have made up yet. Were you on the phone with her all night or something?" she questioned.

"It's hard to be on the phone with someone when they're in the ER getting stitches." Derek scoffed.

"Wait, what?" Ananya's eyes were wide with worry as she moved into the trailer, taking a seat next to him.

"Yeah, she got in between her friend and this other dude when they were about to fight. She took the punch instead, fell, and hit her head," he summed up.

"Fuck! She's like a thug! Like a real thug! Throwing down with guys? Damn, you found yourself a badass," Ananya exclaimed.

"I guess." He sighed. "But she's a badass who still won't talk to me and hasn't returned any of my calls."

"If I got knocked out by a dude, I wouldn't be making any phone calls either," Ananya reasoned.

"True, but she did leave the 'I love you' text on read," Derek said, running his hand through his hair with a sigh.

"Whoa, didn't know you felt that way about her. Damn, D." Ananya was in shock. "But from a girl's perspective, I wouldn't text you back either. I mean, why would she? You don't confess your love to a girl via text. What's wrong with you?" she snapped.

"What else was I supposed to do? She won't talk to me. I figured if she saw the text, she would at least respond," Derek argued.

"If you truly feel that way about her, you need to show her, not just text it, because you say that and the last thing you showed her was you kissing Lexie. I'm just saying," Ananya retorted. "I'll help you fix this mess later, but we gotta get this scene done. Come on."

Derek sighed heavily as he got up and followed Ananya to the set. He knew she was right. He had to show Taryn how he felt, and he'd spend the entire summer doing so if he had to. He was going to fix things with her and win her heart back if it was the last thing he did. With the help of his castmates too, he knew he could make Taryn his by the end of the summer.

When Derek got back to his trailer, there was still no call from Taryn. But as he opened his text messages, one flashed at him, giving him hope that things would be okay.

"I'm sorry I haven't been responding to you. Yes, I did get your messages, but Hawai'i has been hectic since I got back, and quite honestly, I didn't really know how to face you after the letter I left for you. I hope you found it because if not, this text won't make any sense. For now, I just need some time and space, so I won't be responding to anything after this message. I need to focus on me while I'm home, okay? I hope you understand. But I promise you, we'll talk when I get back to the Bay this summer. I'm sorry again." (Taryn)

If time and space was what she needed, he would give her just that. Derek smiled at the text despite knowing he wouldn't hear from her for at least two more weeks. But he couldn't wait for time to pass. Hopefully, being in the same city this summer would help them work on things together, and he could get her to fall in love with him all over again.

25

Lewis

George dropped him off at the Hawaiian Airlines terminal. He walked in, and the white flooring shocked his eyes. The crowded lobby still seemed lifeless with the new stands for self-check-ins. He pulled his reservation up on his phone and began to type his confirmation number into the screen. Just as he was finishing checking in and his documents were printing, he felt someone's arms wrap around his waist, a face suddenly resting on the dip in his back between his shoulder blades.

"I'm sorry," the familiar voice said. It was Taryn.

"No, I'm sorry," he said, grabbing his ticket and turning to her. "I should've given you that letter a long time ago. I'm sorry I wasn't man enough to admit I had feelings for you, Ti."

"It's water under the bridge," she replied, smiling up at him. "But we'll talk more later, okay? You still owe me dinner when I get back to the Bay."

"Deal," he said, leaning down and kissing her on the forehead. "Wait, how'd you know I was over here?"

"Mal. I asked her what time your dad was bringing you here," Taryn replied. "And my parents' plane lands in about an hour, so it worked out perfectly. I couldn't let you leave without making sure we're okay."

"Of course we are," Lewis replied, squeezing her.

"Promise? I don't want to have lost my friend over some silly old letter when I just got you back in my life," she mumbled into his shoulder.

"I'm not going anywhere." Lewis smiled.

"Liar," Taryn teased. "You're leaving for California in a few hours."

"Stop." Lewis laughed, looking down at his ticket. "I don't board for another two hours. How about I drop my bag off and we go downstairs, grab some coffee, and I'll keep you company until your parents land?"

"I could go for some coffee." Taryn smiled as he offered his elbow out for her to grab.

She graciously snaked her arm through his elbow, and they walked together through the terminal. They weren't on perfect terms and still had plenty to talk about before figuring out where they stood with their friendship, but this was a great start to a hopeful summer for the both of them, regardless of what the future would hold.

26

Taryn

It was the last Wednesday of school, the last day of finals for her students before summer break. Almost two weeks had passed since the roughest week of her life. She thought back to the emotional rollercoaster she had been on and was glad things were slowly getting back to normal. Gradually, she was also preparing for her summer move to San Francisco in five days, not just packing but prepping herself mentally. If one week of being in San Francisco set all that off in her life, she had to be ready for what ten weeks in the Bay Area would have in store for her.

The morning was typical. Her alarm went off at 5:00 a.m. for her to get ready. Leaving the house by 5:45 a.m., she called in her mobile order to Starbucks and picked it up on her way to the school. Stopping by the front office, she signed in before moving her car to the back parking lot. Taryn's favorite time of day was the morning. Getting there a little under two hours before the first bell rang, before classes began, gave her a sense of peace and calm. It was a time where she could sit and just enjoy being in her classroom, a room that she had worked so hard to earn. This gave her time to prep whatever she needed to, listen to some music, and give her own students a place to eat breakfast if they got dropped off early.

Her phone read 6:15 a.m., right on time. She sat in her car, sipping her coffee and giving herself five more minutes to listen to the joke of the day on the radio. Suddenly, a cold-blooded scream filled her ears as her moment of peace was shattered. She put her coffee down and quickly jumped out of the car, her eyes frantically scanning the empty parking lot for a face to put with the scream. There were only two of her other coworkers here already, and she was beginning to worry something had happened to one of them.

The scream pierced through the stillness of the morning air once more as she spun around and ran toward it. As she got closer, she could hear sobbing between the shrill sound that now rang in her ears. As she turned the corner of the ninth grade office building, another scream echoed in the air. This time, it was her own.

Her heart threatened to jump out of her chest, and her throat was unable to form words. She froze for a second, staring at the scene before her. A student, Marvin, a boy she had taught that was now in the eleventh grade, was hanging. The noose around his neck was raw with blood as his body seemed to float there, lifeless. Standing in front of her was another teacher, Sarah, a first year teacher who was frozen in place by the horrid scene.

With adrenaline pumping, life made its way back into her body, and Taryn sprang into action. She pushed past Sarah, jumped up on the bench next to the tree, and grabbed onto the boy's body, using all her strength to lift him up by the waist.

"Sarah! Help me!" Taryn screamed.

Unable to get past what she saw, Sarah stood there, frozen and sobbing, leaving Taryn to attempt to help Marvin all on her own.

"This isn't working!" Taryn sobbed on a yell.

"What the fuck?" yelled Garrett, a tenth grade teacher. He had just turned to corner, coming into work for the day, and stumbled upon the terrifying scene.

"Garrett! Help me! I can't get him down!" Taryn screamed through her tears from across the walkway.

Garrett sprinted over, pulling out scissors from his schoolbag before dropping the rest of his belongings on the ground. Tiptoeing, he tried to reach the top of the rope and cut, but the scissors were too dull.

"Damnit!" he exclaimed as Taryn began to struggle to hold the weight of the boy's body.

"Garrett, switch with me!" Taryn exclaimed. "Hold him up. I have a knife in my car. Sarah, snap the fuck out of it and call 911! Or call the office! Call someone to come help!"

Everyone maneuvered around each other based on Taryn's orders. Her heart pounded in her chest, her breath heavy. Taryn sprinted with all her might to her car, yanked her pocket knife out of her glove compartment, and ran back to them.

Garrett was holding the boy's body up with one arm while bracing the boy's neck up with the other. Sarah was on the phone with 911 as security guards on the golf carts swung around the building at full speed. Taryn jumped up on the bench next to Garrett and, with a few back-and-forth motions, cut the rope from the tree.

A security guard helped Garrett slowly lower the boy's body to the grass while others set up a perimeter around the ninth grade area. Taryn dropped onto her knees next to Marvin's lifeless body. She took his cold hand in hers as Garrett and a security guard started CPR, every chest compression jerking Marvin's hand in hers. Taryn felt dead inside. All the blood seemed to have drained from her body; the warmth of the tears falling from her eyes was the only sign of life within her.

It seemed as if hours had passed before the ambulance got to them. Everyone seemed to move in slow motion as she continued to sit there, holding Marvin's hand.

"Taryn, let go," a voice told her. It seemed to whisper from far away. "Taryn, let go."

Garrett knelt down next to Taryn, his hand slowly prying hers from holding onto Marvin. Taryn looked at him, her eyes swollen from crying, her cheeks stained with her tears.

"Taryn, let go…please," Garrett repeated as he helped her up from the grass. "Let the EMTs take care of him. It'll be okay."

The two of them stepped back and continued to stare on as the EMTs feebly tried to pump life back into Marvin's body. Taryn clenched her eyes shut, silently hoping that when she opened them, it was just a dream. But it wasn't. The ninth grade vice principal, Ronnie, softly shook Taryn by the shoulders to get her attention and ushered her into the office nearby. Garrett followed behind, wiping his own tears.

As they entered the office, it was chaos. The clerk was on the phone, counselors were making calls and running around, and the police and firefighters were going in and out. Taryn could hear Sarah in one of the office rooms crying as she gave her statement to a police officer. Taryn was on autopilot, moving through it all without control over herself.

"Here, Ti, sit," Ronnie said, pulling out a chair for Taryn. "Please."

Taryn sat without a word. Garrett pulled out a chair next to her. The both of them were still in shock over what just happened.

"Thank you," Taryn sobbed, suddenly turning to Garrett. "Thank you for helping me. I couldn't…I couldn't get him down on my own."

Dropping her head to her knees, Taryn broke down.

"Shhhh, it's okay." Ronnie began to sob as well as he knelt down next to Taryn.

Garrett, unable to find the right words, dropped his head and sobbed, reaching out a hand to rub Taryn's back. Just then, a knock on the door pulled their attention back from the depths of their sorrow.

"Hi, I'm officer Christian. I—" he started.

"He's going to be okay, right? Marvin? We got to him on time?" Taryn sobbed, her eyes pleading for hope.

"I'm sorry, ma'am. He's gone. Based on rigor mortis, he was already dead for about four hours before you found him," Officer Christian said with empathy.

Taryn fell back into the chair, unable to believe what she just heard. Her head was throbbing, and tears burned her cheeks freely, her mind unable to get past her cloud of grief and wrap itself around the fact that her student was gone. She cried silently, unable to utter any sound, the pain in her clenching every in of her throat, the pain, threatening to crush her heart from the inside out.

"I can't imagine how tough this is on you right now, but we found this in his pocket. We're not supposed to do this, but I feel like you need to read this before we bag it as evidence. I'll come back for it," Officer Christian said as he handed a folded paper to Ronnie.

"Thank you, Officer," Ronnie said as he opened the paper and began to read. Taryn watched as tears rolled down Ronnie's face. "Ti, you need to read this."

She took the paper slowly, her hands shaking. Taryn looked at a letter that Marvin wrote. Garrett scooted in next to her and read the letter with her. The breath was sucked from her lungs as her insides crumbled seeing the letter addressed to her.

Dear Ms. Ti,

If you're reading this before getting a chance to yell at me for even thinking of what I'm about to do, then I'll already be in heaven…hopefully, and I apologize. Even if I end up in hell, it would be a whole lot better than being on earth right now. I know it seems silly to address this to just you, but you're the only one who has ever understood me, and I know, I just know it, that you'll be one to find me. So please let me explain.

Let me start by saying I'm so sorry. I'm sorry for giving you such a hard time in all the time you've known me. I'm sorry for not being a better student. I'm sorry now for not being strong enough to deal with life anymore. I'm sorry I let you down and for not being there for you to see me walking at graduation. But thank you. For being a mom to me, for always listening to me without judging me, for understanding, for truly caring about me as a person, not just because you had to since I was your student. Thank you for always seeing the best in me and encouraging me, even when I didn't believe in myself. Just thank you for everything. I wouldn't have made it through ninth grade or this far in life at all without you. You're the closest thing I ever had to a mother, and you're the only one that I care to explain myself to.

Since I know it'd be you to find me, I want you to know that I chose this location because it was in the ninth grade with you, and the whole ninth grade staff, that I actually felt loved and I felt like I had a real family for the first time in my life. I'll never forget that and will always appreciate all of you for it. You truly made me feel like I had a family again, and I'll forever be grateful to you guys.

As you know, life for me has been rough. Since my mom died when I was seven, my dad has either been angry, drunk, or unconscious. It's one of the three, never anything else. You know I've been working on the days I don't have college class after school, and I've been using my paychecks to help with rent and whatnot since Dad's been calling in sick to work more and more. Today was the last straw for me. Dad beat me to a pulp and threatened to throw me out if I didn't give him the paycheck I earned so he could buy beer. I told him it was for rent, and he blanked out and started hitting me.

He said I was good for nothing and that his life would be better if I were dead. He said it was my fault that my mom died, and maybe if I had died instead, my mom would still be alive and he would still be happy. Is this true? I keep trying to tell myself that it's not. That Dad's just drunk again, but it's hard not to believe him. Aren't we supposed to respect our parents enough to believe what they tell us?

His words have been haunting me since he passed out, exhausted from using me as a punching bag again, and I can't get past it. I'm tired of this already. I'm just tired of trying when nothing is changing, nothing is getting better. Death is my only escape. I know it's the coward's way out, but when you feel like you have no other choices, isn't it brave to be able to make that hard decision? For yourself? I'm so sorry, and thank you again for understanding. I'll watch over you guys and make sure the ninth graders stay in line.

Love, Marvin

Taryn slumped onto the floor crying, clenching onto the seat of the chair and the edge of the desk as if they were the only things left holding her to the earth. Garrett sat next to her crying as Ronnie walked outside, sobbing and needing to get some fresh air. The pages of the letter floated down to the ground as Taryn's world seemed to crumble down with them. She thought she was broken before, but the death of her student, and then this letter, obliterated what little composure she had left.

Officer Christian came back into the room, pain filling his own eyes. It was never easy dealing with the death of a child, but a death of this manner was even more so difficult for all those involved. Bending down and picking up the letter, he sighed heavily.

"Whoever this Ms. Ti was, she sounds like an amazing teacher. We need more like her to impact our kids' lives. Make them feel like they're not alone like this, you know?" Officer Christian said, trying to steady his voice.

"She's Ms. Ti," Garrett choked out, nodding toward Taryn as he rubbed circles of comfort into her back.

"Wow, he knew you'd be the one to find him?" Officer Christian sighed. "I'm so sorry for your loss. You must have impacted him in amazing ways. I'm truly sorry."

Taryn couldn't speak. She just shook her head and rested it down on the seat of the chair as tears continued to pour from her eyes. She didn't even know humans had this much water in their bodies that would allow for her to be crying this long.

The rest of the morning was a blur. Finals got canceled, and students were sent on summer break early. Teachers had an emergency staff meeting to go over what happened and plan a vigil for Marvin, shooting to do it by the end of the week before everyone left on vacation. A generalized grading scale was given so teachers could close their grade books and finish the year early as well. Taryn avoided contact with everyone at all costs. Understanding the trauma she had been through, Principal Del allowed her to stay cooped up in the ninth grade office all day, out of sight and tucked away from the rest of the staff. Garrett stayed with her, both still unable to talk but silently comforting each other. Some of their friends, other teachers, came in to give comforting words and hugs, but Taryn couldn't find it in her to respond. She was like a zombie as she waited for the day to be over so she could go home.

Taryn was still on autopilot as she walked through the crowd of news cameras to the parking lot. She sat in her car and looked down to see her coffee from this morning was still there. Resting her head on the steering wheel, she clenched her eyes shut. She was all cried out and had no tears left, feeling dry and empty inside.

When she got home, she entered her house quietly. Tiana and Noah, who were aware of what happened, sat silently as they watched her walk to her room, both unsure of what to say, if there was anything anyone could say to comfort Taryn. Dropping everything on the ground of her bedroom as she entered, Taryn turned to her bathroom and began to fill her bathtub with hot water.

As it filled, she jumped in the shower, turning the hot water on full blast, letting the beads of water burn her skin in an attempt to wash the memory of today away. Going through the motions, she shampooed and conditioned her hair and washed her body before jumping out of the shower. She dropped a bath bomb into the tub, stepped in, and turned off the faucet. Taryn lay in the tub, feeling numb despite the burning hot water. The sound of the bath bomb fizzing as it dissolved in the water was the only sound that filled the space. Tears started welling in her eyes again, slowly dropping from her eyes as she remained motionless, feeling utterly helpless, alone, and permanently broken. She thought she knew about pain before, but in comparison to what she felt now, she realized she knew absolutely nothing.

27

Derek

In five days, Taryn would be back in the Bay Area, and Derek couldn't be more excited. He had been giving her the space she had requested in her last text, so he was nervous to see her again. But it was a good nervous, more like butterflies in your stomach. They had just wrapped filming for the day, and the cast was on their way to have dinner together when he got a text from Nathan with a link to a Hawai'i breaking news story and nothing more. As he got into Jared's car, he clicked on the link, and his heart sank.

Teen Commits Suicide on School Campus

> At 6:00 a.m. today, the body of eleventh grader Marvin Thompson was found hanging from the tree in the ninth grade area of Westcoast Secondary Academy. The student was found by teachers Taryn Okata, Garrett Wong, and Sarah Hamilton. Hamilton alerted authorities as Okata and Wong removed Thompson's body from the tree and began CPR. Thompson was said to have had a suicide letter explaining the reasoning of his death. The school has closed early for summer in light of this, and a vigil for Thompson will be held by the school this Friday on the football

field. We will keep you updated as the investiga-
tion into this tragedy unfolds.

"What the fuck?" Derek suddenly exclaimed, scaring Ben and
Jared.

"What's going on?" Jared asked, concerned, glancing over as he
drove them down the street.

"It's Taryn. I need to call her," Derek replied.

"Wait, what happened?" Ben asked, reaching from the backseat
and taking Derek's phone from him.

"Ben!" Derek shouted as he turned to try and grab his phone
back.

"Brooo! What the fuck! That happened today? And Taryn found
the body?" Ben exclaimed, quickly reading through the article still up
on Derek's phone.

"Yes! Now give me back my phone. I need to call and make sure
she's okay," Derek argued.

"I can guarantee she's not okay, bro. What the fuck," Ben continued in shock.

"Taryn found a body? What body? Will someone tell me what
the fuck is going on?" Jared yelled frantically.

"A student hung himself at her school! Taryn found the body,
had to do CPR and everything!" Ben summed up.

"What the fuck?" Jared exclaimed as he pulled over into the
nearest parking lot. "Dude, is she okay?"

"I don't know!" Derek yelled as he jumped out of the car and
started calling Taryn.

Ananya and the rest of their cast members pulled into the parking lot next to Jared.

"Yo, this isn't where we were eating," Ananya said as she rolled
down the passenger side window to talk to Jared.

"Shhh! We have a crisis right now," he replied, pointing to
Derek who was pacing on the other side of the car.

"Here, read this," Ben said, rolling down his window after finding the same news article that Derek had. He passed his phone across
the space between the two cars to Ananya.

As she read the article out loud to everyone in the car, all of their mouths dropped, and their eyes bulged open. Ananya was barely able to get through the last few words as the reality of what was going on hit her.

"Wait, this is Derek's Taryn? The Hawai'i Taryn?" Ananya questioned, trying to clarify things for herself.

"Yes," Jared said, glancing in his rearview mirror at an ever-panicking Derek.

"Fuck," Ananya said as everyone grew quiet and waited patiently for Derek to come back to the car.

After fifteen minutes of constantly calling and just getting Taryn's voicemail, Derek's frustration got the best of him, and he threw his phone to the pavement, shattering it into tiny pieces. Derek collapsed against the back of Jared's car and dropped his head into his hands, sobbing. Again, Taryn needed him, and again he couldn't be there for her. Ananya and Jared got out of the cars and slowly walked over to where he had slumped down to the pavement, his phone scattered in tiny pieces around him.

"D, we don't know what to say. How can we help?" Jared asked empathetically, kneeling down next to his friend.

"Let us know how we can help," Ananya added.

Derek just shrugged. He didn't even know what to do right now. As he sat there sobbing, Ananya and Jared began picking up the pieces of his phone.

"Let's start by getting you a new one of these, okay? If your phone is broken, Taryn won't have any way to call you back," Jared reasoned.

"It'll be okay. Whatever you gotta do, we got your back, D. This cast is like a family, and families take care of each other. Remember that," Ananya said, squatting down and resting a comforting hand on his shoulder.

Their producer, Mindy, emerged from Ananya's SUV then. Her face was filled with sorrow as she stared at a distraught Derek sitting on the ground of the parking lot. He was supposed to be the popular heartthrob jock in the series, but right now, he was completely broken, and Mindy knew he wouldn't be able to give his all to filming until he was able to take care of this.

"Derek, go to her," Mindy said, breaking the silence that had built. "We won't get the Derek we all love, and you won't be able to focus on your role until you figure this shit out."

"Huh? What about the scenes we need to film tomorrow? I can't just leave you guys," Derek replied responsibly, looking at her with disbelief in his eyes.

"Yes, you can. We can spare you for a couple of days," she reasoned. "We'll rearrange the shooting schedule and just get all the shots and scenes that you aren't in. We're flexible, and like Anya said, we got your back. Do what you gotta do." Mindy smiled sincerely.

"We all have your back, D. Go to her. We'll hold it down while you're gone, and we can catch all your shots the second you get back," Ben said as he and the rest of the cast emerged from the cars, standing around Derek and showing their support.

"I can't. What about budgeting and sch—-" Derek started.

"Stop making excuses to not face her. She needs you, dummy. We're giving you the pass of a lifetime, D. Take it and just bring us back some Hawai'i snacks," Ananya cut him off.

"Thank you, guys." Derek sighed, his eyes glazing over with tears of appreciation. "You have no idea how much this means to me."

28

Lewis

Lewis was scrolling through his Facebook feed during his lunch break when he found out what had happened. At first, the story that everyone was talking about was this teenager who committed suicide on a high school's campus. But as social media found out more information about the suicide, he saw Taryn's name pop up as one of the teachers who had found the body. Unable to fly home again anytime soon, Lewis was stuck trying to call Taryn, but every call went straight to voicemail, as if her phone were off. He turned to his next best option and called Jazzy.

"Jazzy, did you hear about Ti?" Lewis asked in a panic.

"Yes, I did, and I'm going to swing by tonight. Her mom said she's still at the school and can't leave yet. I'll update you as soon as I talk to her," Jazzy replied before hanging up.

Hours passed, and he still couldn't get through to Taryn. His worry grew to fear, knowing everything she had been through. It was as if life knew she was finally able to start moving on, and it slammed her in the face with yet another obstacle to get over. It was almost midnight in California when Jazzy finally called back.

"Is she okay?" Lewis answered frantically.

"Yes and no." Jazzy sighed heavily. "I don't know, Lewis."

"What do you mean? Did you talk to her?" Lewis asked.

"Physically, she seems okay, but she could barely speak about anything. She was like a zombie," Jazzy replied.

"Did she tell you what happened? Like anything they didn't report in the news? I've been keeping up with the story like crazy on social media, but nothing's confirmed, and everyone is twisting it with their own interpretations of what happened. I was getting pissed because some people were saying it's the teachers' fault that this kid died, for not making him feel more welcome or special. Like what the fuck?" Lewis said angrily.

"Yeah, Taryn saw that. And between people giving their two cents about a situation they know nothing about and others asking her if she was okay, it's like she just snapped. She turned off her phone and threw it in her drawer. It was just too much to deal with," Jazzy explained.

"But she talked to you, right?" Lewis questioned.

"Yeah, sort of. When I asked why she wasn't picking up, she told me what I just told you and then said something about a letter. Apparently, the kid was her former student when he was a freshman, and he wrote to her specifically, saying he knew she'd find him, and he apologized for not being strong enough to deal with life anymore. He said she was the only person that cared about him," Jazzy began on a heavy sigh. "Finding his body didn't break her spirit. It was that letter. Ti kept questioning herself about how her students could speak so highly of her, about her caring and being there for him, when she couldn't save them when they needed her the most. That was the last thing she said before she zoned out. Then she just sat there, face blank, as if she were frozen, repeating over and over again that she couldn't save him. I never saw her like that before, Lewis."

"Like what?" he asked, confused.

"It was as if she were a zombie. No emotion on her face, not moving, not even making crying noises. And she just kept repeating, '*I couldn't save him*' over and over again, like it was a mantra or something. The only sign of emotion was the tears that ran down her face, but it was as if they were just falling from nowhere because her eyes were just glued open and empty," Jazzy detailed.

"Fuck! I wish she would answer her phone," Lewis said, frustrated.

"She doesn't want to talk to anyone. This hit her harder than her divorce from Toby. She was completely despondent. If she was unwilling to talk to anyone about the Toby thing, I'm surprised I even got that little bit out of her after what she went through today. In all our years growing up together, seriously, I've never seen her like that. I'm really worried," Jazzy replied.

"Well, just watch out for her and check in on her when you can, please." Lewis sighed heavily. "And when she gets to the Bay, I got her. I hate that I can't be there for her right now though."

"I got her, Lew. I'm thinking the Bay will do her even better now. She needs to get away for a while, especially after this. This is too much shit for anyone to handle. Being closer to her brother will help too," Jazzy said. "But I'll keep you posted, okay? Just give her some time. She'll come around. I think she's just in shock still, at least for right now."

"I know. Maybe I'll just keep calling until she finally answers. Maybe if I call enough, her phone will turn on by itself," Lewis joked.

"Go for it. But I'll talk to you soon, okay? Bye," Jazzy said as she hung up.

It's one thing to find the body of one of your students, but to have that kind of letter addressed to you, on top of that? Lewis couldn't even imagine how he would feel in that situation, and in that moment, he truly felt sorry for Taryn. She was such a good person. She always cared for others and put everyone else before herself. She didn't deserve to go through any of this! Lewis knew she would need his friendship more than ever this summer, to find herself again and find her way through all this darkness.

29

Nathan

Nathan was distraught as he paced back and forth in their apartment. How much more could his sister handle before she broke? He knew Taryn was one of the toughest women he knew, and she was always the strong one in the family, but she even had a limit, right?

Tiana had blown up his phone yesterday while he was in a meeting until he finally took a second to take her call. After hearing what happened, he explained the situation to his boss and was sent home for the day. His boss gave him the rest of the week and weekend off to fly home and be with his family. He and Sienna had spent all Wednesday afternoon and Thursday morning looking for reasonable flights that they could afford to fly home. With rent being so expensive, it was difficult for them to find a cheap flight at the last minute, and it was driving him crazy.

Taryn not only finding a dead body but the dead body of her student, and having to do CPR on it, was something Nathan couldn't wrap his mind around. Taryn treated all her students like they were her own kids, and she cared for them as such, being there for them through thick and thin, even after they graduated. So for her to lose a student in this manner was probably like losing her own child, especially after the letter her mom briefly told Nathan they had found.

Ti hadn't spoken to the family about anything regarding what had happened, only nodding a silent agreement or shaking her head no when Tiana and Noah would ask her questions. Even when

Nathan called, she didn't answer and wouldn't take his call when he tried to talk to her with Tiana's phone. She hadn't eaten and only came out of her room to grab a glass of water. Taryn had turned her phone off completely, sick of everyone trying to call to see how she was and telling her that in time, things will be okay again, Tiana had explained.

The only person Taryn had spoken to was Jazzy, who had driven there Wednesday night after finding out what happened. All Jazzy could say was she understood where Ti was coming from. Why would you ask if she was okay if you knew she wasn't after what happened? But other than that, Taryn didn't say much, and Jazzy just made sure she took a shower so she could get the grass and dirt off herself from when she did the CPR.

"Fuck!" Nathan exclaimed, frustrated, punching the wall. "How can I take time off to go home to Hawai'i and be there for Ti if I can't fucking afford it?"

"Calm down, Nate," Sienna soothed. "We'll find something. You're just starting out at your company, so of course we're going to be struggling a little right now. It'll work out though. I can dip into my savings if worse comes to worst, okay? We'll figure this out."

"I'm supposed to be taking care of you and Ti and everyone. How can I do that if I literally *can't* right now? I feel so fucking useless!" Nathan punched the wall again, his anger getting the best of him.

"Nathan!" Sienna yelled after him as he suddenly stormed out of their apartment.

He needed some air and space to clear his head. The helpless feeling growing inside was setting his anxiety on fire, and he was on the verge of breaking down himself. His phone started ringing in his pocket.

"I'm taking a walk! I just need to be alone right now!" Nathan yelled into the phone, thinking it was Sienna.

"Nathan?" Derek's voice came through the phone. "I read the news article. Are you guys going home? Have you found a flight to Hawai'i yet?"

"Derek? Hey. No, we haven't. Sienna's still looking, but it's all expensive. I fucking hate this. You read the news article? Don't bother calling Ti. She turned off her phone. She isn't talking to anyone," Nathan explained, the words spilling from him without control.

"Yeah, I figured. I tried calling for fifteen minutes straight and kept getting the voicemail. But I did read the article. I wasn't there for her with Toby, and I need to be there for her now," Derek replied. "My producer gave me until Monday off. They're rearranging the shooting schedule so I can go to her. I'll book your tickets with mine so we're all together, okay? I'm online now, and there's a flight that leaves in four hours. I can meet at your place in an hour, and we can head to the airport, okay? Get packed."

"Derek, I can't let you pay for our flights," Nathan argued.

"Too late. It's already done. I asked Emma for yours and Sienna's info this morning and was just waiting to see if you booked your own flight yet before booking mine. I'll see you guys in an hour. Walk back to your apartment and start getting ready," Derek retorted sternly.

"But, Derek, that's too much," Nathan replied.

"No time for arguing. This is for Ti. No one else. Now hurry up and get ready," Derek shot back.

"D?" Nathan said, his voice breaking.

"Yeah?" Derek replied.

"Thank you." Nathan sobbed, letting out a sigh of relief.

"No problem." Derek sighed before hanging up the phone.

*****

"Babe? Get your stuff packed. Derek will be here in an hour to pick us up, and we'll head to the airport," Nathan said as he swung open the door to the apartment.

"Huh? We didn't book our tickets yet. Are we just going to go and do standby?" Sienna asked, confused.

"Nope. Derek got our info from Emma and booked our tickets once he read the article I sent him about Ti," Nathan replied, opening their carry-on cases and flying clothes in.

"Wait, I thought you sent that to him just so he knows what happened. I didn't expect him to want to fly to her," Sienna said, amazed. "Wow. Derek is earning some brownie points with me. It's about time he is stepping it up for Ti."

"I still don't feel okay with him paying for us though," Nathan admitted. "But I'm desperate. At least we'll have all summer to pay him back."

Sienna nodded her agreement as she jumped in the shower to quickly wash up. Within thirty minutes, the two of them were bathed and had their carry-on bags packed so they didn't have to worry about checking in luggage. They were waiting for Derek to get there. Nathan was growing more and more comfortable with the idea of Derek potentially being with his sister, and it wasn't just because of Derek's generous gesture to fly them to Hawai'i with him. It was because finally, Derek wasn't just saying how much he cared about Taryn, but he was showing it.

Derek swung by within the hour, and they were on their way to the airport. After checking in, they were at the gate. All they had to do was wait to board. All three of them were anxious and unsure about what they would be walking into when they got to Hawai'i. Their flight would land around 10:00 p.m., so as they waited, Nathan sent a message to his mother.

> "Mom, we're at the airport. We'll be landing at
> 10pm. Please pick us up in the 4Runner. Tell Ti
> we're on our way and we love her." (Nathan)

With that, the flight to Hawai'i would be the last moments of peace they'd have until they had to pull it together and be strong for Taryn. Their only worry? Would she let them be strong for her, or would this be the final straw, the thing that would break her forever?

30

Taryn

She peeked out of her room, looking around the living room and kitchen cautiously. Tiana and Noah weren't home. Her uncle had come by the night before, after finding out about what happened and picked up her grandma so the family could deal with helping Taryn face whatever she was going to be going through.

Ti truly appreciated everyone's support but couldn't help but feel like she just wanted to be alone. Her eyes were swollen and burning from crying so much, her head was pounding, and she was so tired, but she couldn't sleep because images of her student hanging in the tree haunted her every time she closed her eyes.

Blue digital numbers shone 8:22 p.m. on the microwave as she meandered her way to the kitchen to make herself a cup of tea. She hadn't eaten anything for almost forty-eight hours, but the only thing that seemed appetizing to her right now was chai tea. She didn't know if it was the smell of the cinnamon in it that could bring her a feeling of Christmas happiness in May, or if the warmth of the tea just soothed her, but it was the only thing that was bringing her some peace during this time. As the water in her pot began to boil, she dropped a tea bag in and turned off the stove for it to steep when the doorbell rang.

"Alexa, show me the front doorbell," Taryn said aloud, her voice scratchy and her throat sore from crying so hard the day before.

"Front doorbell camera," the Alexa in the kitchen chimed back.

Taryn stared at it for a moment before realizing it was her administrators at her door.

"What are they doing here?" Taryn said to herself on a heavy sigh as she went to the door. Opening it slowly, she looked at the two men before her with cautious eyes.

"Hey, Ti, I know it's late but can we come in?" Ronnie asked her gently.

Not saying anything, Taryn shifted to the side and waved them in toward the dining room table.

"I'm not going to ask if you're all right because I know you aren't. So instead, I'm going to ask how you're holding up with everything," Principal Del said as he sat down.

"You weren't answering your phone when we called earlier, so we figured we'd swing by since you live so close to the school," Ronnie explained.

"You're right, I'm not okay. I appreciate you guys coming over to check on me, but I really don't feel like talking to anyone or seeing anyone right now. I don't know how to cope with all of this, and I need to be alone in order to figure that out," Taryn replied honestly. "I'm barely processing, and I can't wrap my mind around it."

"We totally understand, Ti, but that's not the only reason why we're here." Principal Del sighed, looking nervously over to Vice Principal Ronnie.

"Tomorrow we're holding a vigil for Marvin at the school, a private one for faculty and students," Ronnie began. "When we were brainstorming who should speak tomorrow, we realized it needed to be someone close to the kids, someone who has impacted them, whether they taught them or not. Someone the kids trust and will listen to and have respect for."

"Someone like you," Principal Del finally ushered.

Taryn melted back into her chair, her mouth agape in shock. This could not be happening. She could barely get out of her bed right now, let alone speak in front of the entire school. What was she supposed to even say?

"Before you say no, please hear us out," Principal Del reasoned. "We all voted for you, and all of the staff who knows you said there's no one else that could do a better job rallying the students together during a time like this."

"Taryn, I know it's going to be hard, and it's asking a lot of you, but don't do it for us. Do it for Marvin, for the kids," Ronnie added. "You pride yourself in always being there for them, and right now they need you more than ever. We all do. Please."

The three of them sat silently for a moment as Taryn seemed frozen in time. She was unsure of what to say or do, but Taryn knew deep inside what needed to be done, no matter how difficult or painful it may be. She couldn't be selfish right now. She had to be there for her students. There was something bigger at play, and she couldn't let them down.

"Okay." She nodded after a long pause. "I'll do it."

31

Derek

Derek was restless the entire flight over to Hawai'i. Despite booking their seats in first class, Derek, Nathan, and Sienna couldn't help but fidget uncomfortably, anxious to get to Taryn's side. It was as if the time on the flight was passing extra slow, and they had to wait helplessly for the tiny plane icon on the screen to pass over the wide blue ocean space. When they arrived, Tiana and Noah were already waiting for them at the curb, and without a moment to spare, they were packed in the car and speeding home.

"Thank you so much for picking us up, Mr. and Mrs. Okata," Derek said.

"Not a problem," Tiana replied. "It was a surprise, though, when we found out it was you that was with them. Nathan didn't specify who *we* were that would be flying home."

"Mom, Derek is the one that paid for us to come home, so ease up, will you?" Nathan defended.

"True, thank you for that, Derek. But don't try playing knight in shining armor because she's in a vulnerable place, okay?" Noah argued.

"I promise, I wouldn't do that to her. I'm just here to make sure she's okay," Derek replied.

The rest of the car ride home was silent. Everyone was absorbed into their own thoughts. Despite the heat coming through the windows, even with the air-conditioning on and the darkness outside,

Derek couldn't help but be amazed by the beauty of Hawai'i. He would definitely need to come back here another time, on better terms, to explore the island with Taryn. One thing he finally understood though was Taryn's obsession with the stars. He stared out of the car window, and the plethora of stars littering the sky had Derek in awe. They looked like glitter scattered and sparkling in contrast against the dark sky.

Forty-five minutes later, and after going around what seemed like endless twists and turns around mountains, the car pulled into the garage of a two-story house. Getting out, he took a deep breath and followed Nathan in.

"Taryn's locked herself in her room since she got home Wednesday afternoon. We'll head upstairs and give you guys some space. Maybe you could finally get her to open up and talk, Nathan," Tiana said, giving them each a hug. "Let us know if you need anything."

"Remember, don't take advantage of her," Noah said jokingly, squeezing Derek on the shoulder. "Her room is technically the guest room, so if you piss her off, you'll be sleeping on the couch out here instead of in there with her."

"Yes, sir." Derek nodded with a smile.

"Good night, guys. Thank you again for getting us," Sienna chimed as Tiana and Noah headed off to bed.

"Babe, give me your stuff and I'll put them away in my room upstairs," Nathan said to Sienna. "Then we can deal with Ti."

After handing her stuff to Nathan, Sienna went over and sat on the couch.

"You can sit, you know?" she said to an awkward Derek.

"Oh, thanks," Derek said, sitting, as he took in the home before him. Pictures of Nathan and Taryn were scattered across the wall and shelves. Even if this was their childhood home that they grew up in, everything seemed unusually new.

"They just renovated," Sienna said with a smile as if she read his mind.

"What are all those medals?" he said, his eyes stopping next to what he assumed were Taryn's high school senior portraits.

"Competition medals for cheer. Taryn was a badass, and her club team was amazing. When we came here for Christmas the other year, Nathan and I picked her up from her old gym. She went in just to get a workout in, and even at her age, she was flipping all over the place, and they were just tossing her in the air like it was normal. She's nuts," Sienna explained. "That picture right there, next to her senior portrait? It's an action shot a photographer got of her getting thrown in the air at her last competition."

Derek just stared in awe at it. He knew she cheered before, but not to that extent. He thought cheerleading was just standing on the sidelines, yelling for a team. Derek was blown away by the level of competitiveness cheerleading could have. As he stared at the photo of her upside down in a flip, he was more so in awe of Taryn.

"So what are you going to say to her? You haven't heard from her for a while, right? And you haven't talked to her since before she left the Bay after graduation, right?" Sienna asked seriously.

"Honestly, I'm not sure. I just need to see her and be near her right now," Derek replied.

"That's creepy, dude," Nathan said, approaching them, causing them all to let out a nervous chuckle.

"You ready to do this?" Sienna sighed as she stood.

"Yep. Just follow my lead. Mom just let me know upstairs. She forgot to tell Ti that we were coming home, and she definitely does not know you're here, D," Nathan said, waving them to follow him as he walked down a small hallway leading to the back of the house.

Derek followed silently behind Sienna as they approached a white door. Slowly, Nathan took the doorknob and knocked gently as he pushed it open.

"Ti?" Nathan said, popping his head into the room before pushing the door open. "What the fuck?"

Suddenly, Nathan swung it all the way open as he stormed in. As Derek walked over them gingerly, peering in, he saw with surprise that the room was empty. The lamp on her nightstand was on, but there was no one in the room at all. Nathan rushed over to the en suite bathroom and shoved the door open frantically as he searched the bathroom for his sister.

"Fuck. She's not here," Nathan said, frustrated.

"Where could she be?" Sienna asked, concerned.

Without hesitation, Nathan pushed past them in the hallway and headed to the front door.

"Come on." He sighed heavily and slid into a pair of rubber slippers before tossing some to Sienna and Derek to borrow. "She's at the beach."

Derek's mind suddenly went back to the conversation they had the first night they met, her secret spot. The place she went to clear her mind and find peace when life was getting overwhelming. The place her friend found her just two weeks ago. Derek suddenly found his body moving in autopilot, following behind Nathan and Sienna, who were speed walking down the street toward the traffic light. Even if they knew where she was, it didn't make the sense of panic go away. Something had to be wrong to pull her from the safety of her room and out and onto the beach in the middle of the night. After crossing the street and treading across the grass, their feet finally hit the sand. The sound of the waves crashing on the reef matched the crunching of sand beneath their feet as their pace quickened. Derek's lungs began to burn in his chest as they made their way across the beach.

"Right there. Can you see her?" Nathan said as he pointed to this huge smooth boulder while they tracked through the sand. "Fuck, she had to do this on the one night they don't have the tiki lights on!"

"There! I see her!" Sienna exclaimed as a cloud moved across the sky, letting a sliver of moonlight shine down on the beach.

"Does she see us?" Derek asked as he stared at Taryn, who was sitting with her legs crossed as she stared out toward the ocean.

"No, it's too dark out and the ocean usually drowns your voice out. She won't see or hear us until we're closer," Nathan explained.

As they got closer to her, the moonlight seemed to kiss her face, trying to comfort her as tears twinkled on her cheeks like the stars in the sky. He saw her cry before, but the pain that was written across her face was different this time. This was a deeper, unexplainable pain that Derek couldn't begin to comprehend. It made his heart shatter in his chest seeing her this way. Taryn sat there silently. The tears just streamed down her cheeks, her body still.

"Taryn?" Nathan yelled as he approached the edge of the boulder. "What are you doing out here?"

Startled, Taryn's body jerked back as her legs flew up from under her, and her body tumbled off the boulder and into the sand. Her slippers flew from her feet through the air like shooting stars. Sand kicked up everywhere.

"Shit," Nathan said, rushing with Sienna to help his sister up while Derek pulled out his phone's flashlight to find exactly where she fell. "Watch your head!"

"You're home?" Taryn sighed, confused, looking at Nathan as if he were a figment of her imagination while laying on her back in the sand.

"Yes. You need family around you right now, so of course we're here," Nathan replied soothingly as he helped Taryn up and guided her to sit on the boulder.

"We heard what happened, and I know we can't do much, but we needed to be here for you, Ti. We love you," Sienna added, sitting next to her and pulling her into a hug.

Taryn still looked frozen in time, lifelessly sitting there as if her brain was unable to comprehend anything at the moment. Nathan glanced at Derek and nodded toward Taryn, silently urging him to speak up.

"We're all here for you, Taryn," Derek said, clearing his throat as he stepped from the shadows.

"Derek?" Taryn said, surprised, her voice breaking as she stood up slowly to face him.

"Hey." He sighed with a weak smile, unsure how she would react seeing him.

Suddenly, Taryn's body crashed into his as she jumped into his arms, wrapping her own around Derek's neck as she broke down sobbing. All he could do was squeeze her to him, grateful to have her in his arms again. His heart pounded in his chest, threatening to break free with happiness. Derek breathed her in as he shut his eyes, savoring the feel of her in his arms once again.

"Wow, Ti. So you don't talk to him for over two weeks and he gets a hug? I see how it is," Nathan teased, smiling on seeing his sister and Derek wrapped up in each other.

"You're here? In Hawai'i?" Taryn sobbed into his neck, refusing to let him go. "What about filming?"

"Nathan told me what happened, and I knew we had to be here for you. So we booked the first flight out that we could find," Derek replied. "My producer even told me to come to you."

"I really like this guy, Ti. He booked us in first class," Nathan said jokingly with a wink as he nudged his sister.

"Thank you, guys!" Taryn sighed with a smirk. "I can't believe you two are here too!" she said, turning her attention to Nathan and Sienna, finally releasing Derek and pulling them both into a hug.

"Finally, we're not invisible." Nathan laughed, hugging her. "Even if we would've seen you in a few days, it's still good to see you already. How you holding up?"

"As best as I can, I guess. I don't really know. It all doesn't seem real yet." Taryn sighed as she sat back down. "I'm trying to clear my head and pull myself together before I need to talk to all the kids tomorrow."

"Wait, what?" Nathan asked. "What do you mean talk to all the kids?"

"I got asked to speak at the vigil tomorrow. The school feels like I'm the only one the kids will listen to. Not just because I was there and found his body but because they know I have a good relationship with the kids, to the point that they'll actually listen to me when I talk," Taryn replied, sighing heavily as she stared out at the ocean.

"And you're going to do it?" Sienna asked.

"I have to," Taryn said sitting back down. "For myself and for the kids."

"Well, whatever you have to do, know that we'll be there supporting you. We got you, Ti," Derek said as he sat down next to her, his arm wrapped around her.

"Thanks." Taryn smiled. "That means a lot to me."

The four of them remained in silence as Taryn closed her eyes and took a deep breath of the saltwater in the air. Derek watched as she seemed to lose herself in the sound of the waves crashing on the reef, her toes digging into the sand as she hung her feet off the side of the boulder. She looked up to the sky, and it was as if Taryn searched the millions of stars above for strength.

"Calming, isn't it?" Taryn sighed to no one in particular. "I'm glad I came home when I did. I wouldn't be able to deal with all of this as a stranger in a new city. The comfort of home is the only thing holding me together right now."

"Home will always be here to center you, but we'll be right by your side wherever you go to support you, Ti. Especially when you come to San Fran for summer, okay? We got you. Don't doubt that," Nathan assured her.

"I know." She sighed with a smile. "Let's head back. I need to try and sleep tonight if I have to speak tomorrow. I don't gotta be there until ten, but not sleeping for forty-eight hours has taken its toll on me. I don't need to add dark circles to the red puffiness of my eyes."

Taryn stood up on a sigh and began to walk back toward the road bordering the beach's parking lot. Nathan, Sienna, and Derek stood there in shock. Taryn was suddenly alive, moving as if she had purpose in her life. It was a strange change that contradicted the zombie-like Taryn that Tiana and Noah described.

"Ti? You okay?" Nathan asked cautiously as they started to follow her.

"Yeah, I just have something to focus on now. Speaking tomorrow will distract my mind from the images of my student hanging that I can't seem to get rid of. So I'm just excited to lay down. Hopefully, thinking about speaking will give me a small window of peace so I can get some sleep tonight," Taryn said confidently.

Everything about that statement was wrong. It raised so many red flags, but not wanting to trigger Taryn any further, the three of them remained quiet and simply followed her home.

"Don't forget to wash your feet before you go to bed, guys. The sand is dirty," Taryn said with a smile as Nathan and Sienna headed up the stairs to bed.

She looked to the couch. Tiana and Noah had already laid a blanket and pillow out for Derek. But before he could settle in, Taryn scooped everything up and headed for her room at the end of the hall.

"What are you doing?" Derek asked cautiously.

Taryn ignored his question, opened her room, and threw the pillow and blanket on the ground on the side of her bed. She disappeared into the bathroom and emerged with a towel and handed it to him.

"Go and shower really quick. I'm going to get us some tea, and we're going to talk," she said sternly, not leaving him any room to oppose. Derek nodded as he headed into her bathroom to shower.

32

Taryn

Taryn set two cups of chai tea onto her dresser and headed to the doorway of her bathroom to see if Derek was done showering yet. The steam from the hot water filled the bathroom, and the smell of berries invaded her nose. Taryn chuckled to herself at the thought of Derek smelling like a girl after using all her products.

"Ti? Is that you?" Derek said, popping his head out of the shower, his brown curls matted against his forehead.

With his hair wet, his skin glistening in the dim light of her mirror, and his chiseled jawline, his handsome looks sent butterflies fluttering across Taryn's tummy. She couldn't help but tilt her head and stare for a bit, biting her bottom lip as the need to taste him consumed her mind.

"Ti? You okay?" Derek said, wiping his face with his hand so he could see her better.

She walked over to the shower without a word. She took the sight of him in, eyeing him from head to toe. His hands shot down in front of him to cover up as her eyes hovered at the bulge hardening behind them. A nervous look passed over Derek's face as Taryn soaked in the sight of him, naked in her shower.

"What are you doing?" Derek sighed.

"I need a distraction," Taryn said suddenly, yanking her top off over her head, exposing herself, and stepping into the shower with him before he could oppose.

Derek swallowed hard as he was now the one staring at her, half naked before him. Before he could say anything, Taryn's hands were cupping his face as she tippy-toed to kiss him. Her lips collided with his, her tongue pushing past his lips, her breathing becoming hard. Without breaking their kiss, Taryn quickly rid herself of her shorts and panties, tossing them to the floor outside of the shower.

Walking him backward under the water, Taryn's hands moved from his face down to the nape of his neck, each twist of her tongue drenched in more than just sexual desire. She was trying to get lost in him. He gave in, wanting her just as bad. Derek threw his arms around her waist, his hands hungrily moving up and down the length of her back as he pulled her closer. The hardness of his shaft pulsed for her as it rubbed against the silkiness of her stomach.

"Ti, wait," Derek said, breathless, pulling away and bringing Taryn's sexual tension to an abrupt halt. "No. I can't do this with you. Not until we talk first."

"Why?" Taryn said, shocked. "We've done it before. Please, Derek. I just need a distraction right now. Let me get lost with you." Taryn tried to pull him toward her again, but his strength prevented her from budging him at all.

"Come here," Derek directed as he sat on the floor of her shower, the hot water still falling around them. He pulled her onto his lap, harnessing all the strength in him to maintain self-control as the roundness of her behind slid across his length.

"Derek." Taryn sighed, frustrated, as she shrugged her shoulders on a huff.

"Ti, I told you. I can't do this with you until we talk," Derek urged.

"We can talk *after*," Taryn retorted, hiding her face in the crook of his neck, kissing him softly, trying to distract him. Her hands moved wildly across his muscles as if she couldn't get enough of the feel of him.

"No. I need to get this off my chest now. You can't just leave me with that letter, not let me explain myself, and then disappear." Derek hesitated for a moment and took a deep breath before he continued. "You can't do that...especially when I'm falling in love with you, Taryn. I care too much about you to do anything with you yet, until you let me explain."

Stunned by his words, Taryn sat up and stared at his face. He was dead serious, and the furrowing of his brow showed that she wasn't going to get her way until she listened to whatever it was he had to tell her.

"Ti, I love you," Derek said, one hand cupping her face as the other eased on her hip. "I don't care if you think I'm crazy because we barely know each other. But I know what I'm feeling. And no, it's not because you said you were feeling that way first in the letter you wrote that tore my world apart. If anything, you telling me how you felt in the letter just confirmed to me how I felt."

"What about Lexie?" Taryn said, her heart squeezing in her chest as her eyes began to glaze over with tears. "I saw you guys kiss that day. How can you say that you love me if you aren't done with her yet?"

"Lexie lied her way onto our set. She was getting married that weekend and wanted one last fling before she did. I was just caught in her crossfire. That kiss meant nothing to me," Derek said seriously, pulling Taryn closer to his face, to the point she could feel his breath on her skin, sending a tingling sensation down her spine.

"How am I supposed to believe any of that? That an off-and-on relationship with her for over ten years, since high school, is suddenly nothing to you? And that our short fling was actually love?" Taryn scoffed, pulling her face away from his hand and standing up, leaving him to sit on the floor alone. She could see Derek tense under her stares, the hurt at her disbelief clear in his eyes.

"You don't have to believe anything you don't want to. If I were you, I wouldn't believe me either." Derek sighed, looking up at her.

"So why are we even having this conversation? Can't we just call our time together in SF what it was? That it was just a fling?" Taryn spat with venom in her tone.

"Ti! It wasn't just a fling for me. The more time I spent with you, the more I needed to just be around you. These last few weeks without you talking to me has been killing me!" Derek retorted, standing so they were face-to-face. He grabbed her arms so she wouldn't run from him again.

"Don't you mean the more time you spent *in* me, the more you wanted?" Taryn scoffed as she pushed off his chest, breaking free from his grip and exiting the shower.

"Fuck," Derek said as he turned off the shower. Wrapping the towel she had placed for him around his waist, he followed her into the bedroom. "Ti, that's not fair."

Taryn yanked her towel from the top of her dresser and wrapped it around her body angrily. Derek had better watch his next comments because her floodgates were about to break and unleash the built-up pain she had been keeping locked inside, and it would all come crashing down on him.

"Ti, will you just stop for a second and look at me?" Derek said as he grabbed her, turning her to face him.

"What?" she snapped, her face emotionless. Only her eyes showed the glimmer of pain she felt deep in her soul, like the tip of an iceberg peeking out from the water.

"I don't know what I can say to make you believe me. But I love you. Not Lexie, *you*! The time I got to spend with you in SF, short or not, meant more to me than a decade worth of memories with Lexie! And it's *you* that I need in my life. Ti…please!" Derek pleaded, dropping to his knees, tears flowing freely between them as he wrapped his arms around the lower half of her body, refusing to let her go.

"You're right. I don't believe you. If someone who claimed to love me for so long, someone who married me and promised a life with me could suddenly just stop…how can I believe that a complete stranger would love me?" Taryn said coldly. "That's what we are, right? We don't really know each other. So how can you say you love someone that you don't know over someone you have a history with, Derek? Please tell me because I feel like I'm going crazy right now," Taryn said dropping her gaze to him, a stray tear falling from her eye.

Derek's brown eyes stared up at her in shock. This was obviously not how he expected this conversation to go. But she was a little firecracker, and she was smart to boot, so he wouldn't have expected anything less than a fight to keep her in his life. Unable to respond just yet and searching his mind for the right words to say, Taryn continued.

"Look at Lewis too. You were right to have been jealous. Apparently, he did love me all those years ago. But he didn't love me enough to stop me from getting married to someone else. No matter how much he claimed to have loved me back then, it still wasn't enough for him to tell me how he felt. And now? We'll forever be just friends because too much time has passed and we're not the same people anymore. Yet by trying to be his just his friend, I might be hurting the only guy outside of my family that truly cares for me, that has never failed to be there for me," Taryn said, tears welling in her eyes, her breath catching. "I'm such a horrible person. How could anyone love me?"

"Ti, stop, please," Derek said gently, standing up, wrapping his hands around her arms, and pulling her closer to him. He leaned down to be eye-to-eye with her, their noses practically touching.

"No. You wanted to talk, so please let me finish," she said before he could interject anything else. She pulled away from him and stepped back. She was a completely broken human being that was barely able to stand in front of him. "And my students. Regardless of their home lives or how rough they are around the edges when they start the year with me, they are all amazing good kids that just need someone to show them they are loved and cared for. That's why even after they leave me for the year, they know my door is always open if they ever need anything. Whether it's someone to vent to or a place to have lunch, even help with college applications, I'm there because so many of them don't have that at home. But it wasn't enough. He knew I loved and cared for him like a son, just like I did with all my former kids, and he still hung himself because I wasn't good enough. I failed him. I fail everyone around me."

Taryn's world started spinning, and her breathing becoming erratic. Her knees gave out, and she crumbled to the floor in a ball, crying. Derek was over to her in a heartbeat, peeling her off the ground and cradling her in his lap as he rocked her back and forth.

She shook in his arms with body-wracking sobs as a tidal wave of emotions swallowed her.

"Shhh. It's okay," Derek said softly, kissing her hair.

"I couldn't save him," Taryn repeated through sobs.

"Taryn, I can't imagine what you're going through right now, but your job was to be his teacher. Anything more you gave, beyond teaching him, was going above and beyond. You can't beat yourself up for something you had no control over, especially if his home life was a mess," Derek tried to soothe.

"I know that, but the letter…it just…it's too hard to move past." Taryn continued crying. "I've never felt more broken in my life. I don't even know where to start to pick up the pieces again."

"What letter?" Derek asked.

"They found a letter in his pocket, addressed to me. He had talked to me about his childhood before, and the school had intervened with CPS multiple times, but the messed-up system always gave him back to his dad," Taryn said, sitting up so she could face Derek.

"Okay, so he talked about how he couldn't deal with his dad anymore?" Derek questioned.

"Yes." Taryn nodded. "Then he said he chose our area of the school to die because that was the only place he had ever felt truly loved, like he had a real family. And he kept apologizing to me for not being strong enough to deal with it anymore. That he was sorry for letting me down when I was the closest thing to a mom that he had since his real mom passed."

"Oh, Taryn," Derek said, pulling her into his chest, his heart aching for her.

"He didn't need to apologize. I don't even know if I could have lasted that long in his situation. I just hate the thought that in his last moments, he was alone," she cried. "He could have called me instead of writing a letter."

33

Derek

As he sat on the floor with her in his arms, it became all too clear for him. He knew Taryn had one of the biggest hearts of anyone he had ever met, but it was her big heart that was causing herself so much hurt right now. The letter from her student was what broke her, giving her that feeling of helplessness. The thought of her unable to be there for someone she cared about haunted her.

Knowing that her student took the time to write the letter to her was probably killing her on the inside. She said her students knew, present and former, regardless of what she had going on in her life, they could always turn to her and count on her to be there for them when they needed her the most. For this student to feel like he couldn't go to her in his time of need, and the result being his death, it was as if Taryn felt responsible somehow.

"Ti," Derek said into her hair. "He wasn't alone. Like his letter said, he chose that spot so he could be surrounded by memories of the love and family you guys created for him. He was in his happy place when he left."

"Still. I could have saved him, but he didn't give me a chance to," Taryn argued.

"No one could have predicted he would have done this, and I know if you knew that that was his plan, you would have saved him. But no one knew, and it was a choice he made for himself," Derek tried to reason.

"How am I supposed to face my students tomorrow when I've failed one of their own?" Taryn sobbed.

"You'll fail them more if you don't face them," Derek said gently. "They're going to need love and support more than ever tomorrow. The type of love and support that *you* give to them. So for them, you can face anything you need to tomorrow, okay? I'll be by your side the entire time."

Looking up at him with puffy eyes, Taryn nodded. Derek kissed her on the forehead and began shifting to stand up, still holding her in his arms. He walked her over to her bed and placed her down gently. Going to the door, he locked it before returning to the bedside and turning off her lamp.

Derek pulled off the towel wrapped around his waist and dropped it to the floor, exposing every inch of himself to her as his desire drew him closer and closer to Taryn.

"What are you doing?" Taryn asked, wiping her eyes.

"I'm giving you your distraction," Derek replied, his voice heavy with lust.

As he crawled onto the bed, he peeled the towel off her body, exposing her to the moonlight shining in from the window. Her abs were more defined, and her ribs showed a little through her skin after not eating for two days. But she still looked divine. He nudged her legs open with his knee. They moved up the bed as he crawled his way up her body, drawing his fingers slowly up the sensitive inner skin on her thigh. He showered her with kisses over every inch of her as he went.

As his fingers reached her center, he could hear her breath catch. Taking the pad of his thumb, he began to caress her, releasing a small moan from Taryn's lips. He pushed one finger past her entrance, and it slid in with ease. She was soaked for him already, the desire in both of them to be connected once again ripping through them.

"I've missed you so much, Ti," Derek said sexily. His breath was tinged with passion as he stared down at her, watching her writhe under his touch while he pumped his fingers into her at a steady pace. He was slowly building her up to her climax.

"I can't take this, D," Taryn said as she gripped his forearm, her muscles clenching around his fingers.

Seeing her on the edge of her own release, he scooted down and dropped his mouth onto her, sucking gently on her pulsing bud as he plunged two fingers into her depths. He could feel her muscles begin to tighten as all the air was sucked from her lungs. Her eyes rolled to the back of her head as her chest heaved, her breasts looking like luscious mountains before him.

"I want to feel you," Derek sighed, glancing up at her. "I want to bury myself inside of you, Taryn."

"Derek," she moaned as her climax took her. Her head dropped back into her pillows, and her body arching to him as she bit into her bottom lip, gripping onto the sheets around her.

"There she is." He smiled as he guided her down from her release, slowing the pace of his fingers. Her body relaxed into the bed, and he licked her essence from his fingers.

"I want you, Derek," she panted, watching him.

"You do, do you?" he said with a raise of his eyebrows.

"Now," she replied eagerly, propping herself up on her elbows.

Derek couldn't take it anymore. The more he teased her, the more he wanted her. He quickly pushed her down onto the bed and pushed his length into her hungrily, sending her head back into her pillows on a low moan. Taryn's warmth wrapped around him, pulling him deeper. The wet silkiness of her skin against his threatened to push him over the edge before he even started. Resting his forearms on either side of her head, he pushed himself as far as he could go into her, his stomach muscles tensing already as her muscles stretched and molded themselves to fit him. She was perfect, as if she were made just for him.

"I'm going to make love to you tonight." Derek smiled, pulling his face back just enough to look her in the eyes. "I love you, Ti."

"Derek, please...no." Taryn sighed as tears began to well in her eyes. Leaning down, Derek kissed her gently on the nose.

"You may not believe me now, but give me time and I'll prove it to you. I want this forever. You are not just a fling to me," he said with a smile.

Before she could respond, Derek slowly retreated from her warmth before dipping his hips back down, grinding his full length into her as his mouth collided with hers. She moaned into his mouth as her nails dug into his back. As he began to move his hips, Taryn's entire body seemed to awaken, her hips shooting up to meet each advance. Derek's hands caressed every inch of her body as he entered her over and over again, as if his hands were trying to remember everything about her as they got lost in each other's passion. Taryn's senses were on fire as she frantically gripped every inch of Derek's back, as if holding onto him was the only thing holding her to the world right now. As sparks flew, the horribleness of the world around them fell away as their souls seemed to connect. Like a freight train hitting them, they exploded around each other, their releases taking them as their muscles clenched onto each other for dear life. Every inch of their bodies shook and tingled. They were wrapped up together in a breathless dance of desire, slowly working each other down.

"Hey, beautiful," Derek said, resting on top of her body when his breathing finally slowed.

"Hey." Taryn smiled back with a sigh. "I'm sorry I was so distant and didn't let you explain sooner. I guess it's just my way of preventing myself from getting hurt. The farther away you keep someone, the less chances they have to hurt you, right?" She sighed sincerely.

"It's okay," he replied with a sigh as he squeezed her tighter, placing a gentle kiss on her lips. "I understand why you did it. And like I said, you may not believe that I love you right now, or you might be too afraid to let me love you just yet, but know I'm not going anywhere. The more you push me away, the more I'll be there to prove myself to you, Ti. I promise."

Appreciation filled Taryn's eyes as she wrapped her fingers around his neck and pulled his forehead to hers. With a smile, he tilted his head up and placed a kiss on her forehead. He was in awe at the strength of the woman lying beneath him, and he felt so lucky to have her in his arms. She truly was special, and his heart bounded with happiness and hope that they could make it work.

"D?" Taryn said as she looked up at him.

"Yeah?" he replied as he brushed her hair from her face.

"Thank you for coming." Taryn sighed. "Not just in sex," she joked, "but for coming to Hawai'i and bringing Nathan and Sienna with you too. It means more than you know."

"Anytime." He chuckled, smiling down at her. "I told you, I'm not going anywhere."

He turned over and took his place on her bed next to her. She cuddled up next to his body, fitting into his side perfectly like he was the puzzle and she was his missing piece. Laying there with Taryn made Derek so happy. Even if they hadn't had sex, he would've just been happy with having her in his arms again. He finally felt at home and complete by her side, and he wasn't going to ever let her go again.

34

Taryn

Taryn's heart was throbbing in her chest. It was as if each breath barely suppressed the tears that were on the brink of falling from her eyes. Clenching them shut, she tried to center herself and control her breathing. A soft touch on her shoulder pulled her back to the present.

"Thank you for doing this, Ti. You are so strong," Ronnie said with a smile.

"And now to say a few words, Ms. Ti," a student's voice echoed over the speakers on the football field.

"You ready?" Ronnie encouraged.

Taryn nodded and took a deep breath as she stepped out from tunnel entrance of their football field and walked toward the fifty-yard line. It was the longest walk of her life, and everything seemed to move in slow motion despite the chants and claps of the students that seemed to echo so far in the distance. Reaching the middle of the field, she looked up to the stands filled with students, each holding a white balloon with an *M* on it for Marvin. It looked as if she were staring into a sea of clouds as she fought to choke back her tears. As each person entered the stadium that morning, they wrote a message to Marvin on a piece of paper, folded it, and placed inside the balloons before being inflated. At the end of the vigil, everyone would walk onto the field and release them into the sky together.

"We love you, Ms. Ti!" she heard one student yell.

"You da bomb, Ms. Ti!" shouted another.

She hadn't even said anything yet, and tears silently began to fall from her eyes as a small smile of gratitude spread across her lips. Standing center field, looking up at the faces of students and staff alike, in that moment, she felt so proud to be a part of this community, this school, that had become a second family to her. In the announcer's box at the top of the bleachers, she saw her family and Derek sitting with Tiana's friend and old colleague, Principal Del. News cameras and their own video production crew had set up on top of the press box to livestream the vigil on social media. Slowly, the crowd started to settle, and silence fell upon the field. Taking a deep breath, Taryn closed her eyes, digging within herself for strength before gazing on with confidence and speaking from her heart. She began slowly.

"There are no words that can begin to describe the pain and suffering a person has to be feeling to take their own life. My heart aches for Marvin and his family. Not for the fact that he's gone but based on the fact that he felt like he was so alone in that moment that he couldn't reach out to someone for help. Because one thing I do know, you are not alone. None of you are. Even if you may not have the ideal support system, know that there are people out there who care about you. Your family, friends, and your teachers. We are all here for you. So please, don't ever think that you have no one, because you'll always have at least one person to turn to. We push you to be the best you can be, so when the time comes, you are strong enough to face the world, standing tall on your own two feet. Our tough love is our way of showing you that we care, so don't ever think for a second that we don't. Until then, hold each other close, and be each other's support system through this difficult time. We hurt as a community, but we will also grow and thrive from this loss together as well. We will come out of this stronger, wiser, and with more love in our hearts for one another than we could have ever imagined. Do not be discouraged by the pain of today. Hold your heads up high and push through until we reach a stronger tomorrow. And again, if you need anything, whether it be a shoulder to cry on or someone to listen to you and help you through your own struggles, remember we got you guys. We will always be here for you. Thank you."

Tears poured from Taryn's eyes freely as she stood there, a weight somehow lifted from her shoulders and some of the darkness pulled from her chest. The crowd erupted in an array of applause and crying as the students began to be directed to the field with their balloons. As she moved to the side, other faculty members came up to her, hugging her and crying their condolences onto her shoulder and thanking her for the moving speech. Taryn simply nodded acknowledgment to them as she remained frozen in time, a wave of relief washing over her knowing she was able to be there for the rest of her students, even if she couldn't be there for Marvin.

Garrett, her coworker who had helped her get Marvin down from the tree, approached her solemnly, opening his arms for a hug as her face collided into his chest. The both of them got closure on that horrific memory as they cried in each other's embrace.

"You are so strong, Ti," he said between sobs. Taryn just nodded into his chest. Garrett pulled back and handed her a balloon.

"But I didn't write anything." She sighed, confused.

"I'm sure he knows already." Garrett smiled, sniffling.

They walked side by side and headed out toward the middle of the field with the rest of the faculty and students. With the playing of the song "Footprints in the Sand" by Leona Lewis, everyone began releasing their balloons into the air, sending their messages up to Marvin. Taryn sighed heavily to herself and closed her eyes, saying a final silent goodbye to her student, forcing herself to finally let go of all the pain in her life as she released her balloon. It was as if he heard her as a soft breeze kissed her skin, a silent way of letting her know he was okay. Thinking of Marvin, she realized life was too short to hold onto all the hurt she had been through. For him and for her own sanity, she had to move on.

35

Lewis

"Did you see the vigil?" Jazzy's voice boomed over the phone the second Lewis answered.

"Not yet. I'm going to be streaming it on my television. Some of my coworkers heard what happened, so my boss let us take a late lunch, and we're in the office. We're just about to watch it now. Thanks for sending the link to the livestream, Jaz," Lewis said.

"I don't know how Taryn did it. I wouldn't even be able to talk. She was so composed! I'm so proud of her!" Jazzy replied, her voice breaking as if she just finished crying.

"That's Ti for you though. She always pulls it together for everyone else when she needs to. That hasn't changed," Lewis retorted with a note of pride in his voice.

"True." Jazzy sighed. "Well, watch the vigil and call me later, okay?"

"I will," Lewis replied. "Hey, has Ti turned on her phone yet? I want to call and check in on her, but no sense if she still got it off."

"No. But my dad said her brother came home, so I can call him later to see if she's up to talking to anyone else," Jazzy stated. "I think he's staying the weekend, and they're all going to fly back up to SF on Sunday."

"Okay. Keep me posted. Thanks, Jaz," he said, hanging up.

It was killing Lewis that he couldn't talk to Taryn or hear her voice. He just needed to hear her say she was okay, and it would settle his nerves. Even if they had a good conversation at the airport over coffee, everything still felt off between them since she found his letter. It was like she treated him as less than a friend, clearly distancing herself from him because if they were really okay, wouldn't she at least call him to check in? Or to turn to him for comfort?

Lewis wasn't even sure what he was feeling. He knew he still had some type of feelings for her, but after all this time, and not speaking for over ten years, could he still be in love with her? His thoughts were consumed by her since they ran into each other at K-Elements. And after finding out everything that's been going on with her, his worry grew more and more with every minute that passed that he was not able to hear her voice. He had to figure out exactly what he was feeling before she got back to the Bay Area and he had to face her. If she felt something for him, he didn't want to lead her on or hurt her, especially if he didn't feel for her in the same way. Yet at the same time, he didn't want to go in wholeheartedly falling in love with her again if she still only saw him as a friend. His entire psyche was just a mess right now as he seemed to be going in circles, arguing with himself in his head.

"You ready to watch this?" his army buddy Travis said, sitting next to Lewis on the couch and handing him a beer.

"I'm really interested to see who this girl is that's got our boy's balls twisted in a knot," another friend, Joey, said. "But for real though, it's cool of you to support her this way since you can't be there physically."

"Thanks, guys, for being here," Lewis said, typing in the link on the smart TV to the vigil video. "Ti is something else. She deserves as much support as I can give her."

"Well, she's a lucky girl," Travis said, tipping his beer to Lewis before taking a swig.

He clicked play on the video. The vigil started with shots of students entering the field, writing on papers, and putting them in white balloons while the band played the school's alma mater and a classmate sang "It's So Hard to Say Goodbye" by Boyz II Men. Then the principal gave a speech on suicide and numbers to call if they ever felt like hurting themselves before a counselor appeared on the field to give a short eulogy for the student. Three of the student's closest friends gave testimonies, sharing memories they had of him, detailing how he was always caring despite not receiving love and care at home. Finally, Taryn came walking out in black slacks, a black blouse, and black flats. Her hair was pulled back in a clip out of her face, and despite her makeup, you could see the puffiness of her eyes clearly.

"Is that your girl?" Joey asked as he saw Lewis's body language change.

"Yep...that's Ti." Lewis sighed.

"Wow. She's gorgeous even when she's clearly upset," Travis replied bluntly. "She's kind of like a sad puppy you just want to hug, huh?"

"Yeah, kinda." Lewis scoffed with a slight laugh.

As Taryn began to give her speech, the three men fell silent. Tears welled up in all of their eyes as she spoke. You could hear the emotion in Taryn's voice, and her words hit you in the chest like a ton of bricks. Her passion and sincerity could impact anyone who was willing to listen.

"Damn." Travis sighed, sniffling.

"She's tougher than you," Joey joked, wiping his tears.

"Right? I can't even imagine what she's going through right now. I wish I could just hold her, you know?" Lewis admitted through his own sniffles.

"Like a puppy!" Travis exclaimed.

The three men burst out in a depressing laughter, unsure of how else to deal with the fact that Taryn had the three of them, supposedly tough military men, blubbering like girls in the middle of one of their army offices.

"Bro, we gotta pull it together or we'll never live this down with the rest of the unit." Joey laughed, wiping tears from his eyes.

"It's okay. We'll just show them Taryn's speech, and they'll end up crying like us and won't be able to rag on us for it!" Travis replied.

"Thank you, guys. I needed this! You guys are the best," Lewis said on a heavy sigh.

"Bros for life!" Joey barked.

As he rode his motorcycle home from base that night, Lewis couldn't help but think of how much he admired Taryn's strength, for being able to go through what she went through and still stand up tall enough for an entire community to lean on. Despite having the world constantly pound down on her shoulders, she continued to pick herself up and find new ways to move forward. Regardless of what happened between them in the past, Lewis knew she would always hold a special place in his heart, and he would be an idiot to push her out of his life again. This summer would be the start to mending their friendship that once had been broken.

36

Taryn

When one person in their family needed support, everyone would drop whatever it was they were doing and go to that person to help them. After her family had seen the vigil, they flocked to her side. Tiana arranged a potluck dinner on Saturday at their house with Jazzy. They had a family dinner so everyone could get to see Nathan again, even if it was secretly a way for them to show they supported Taryn as well.

Tiana, being one of six, aunts, uncles, and an endless stream of Taryn's cousins and their kids filled the house, the garage, and the backyard. It was a calming chaos that was part of why Taryn loved her family so dearly. What was more so endearing was the way her family took to Derek so quickly. After Toby, Taryn feared they wouldn't take to anyone she brought home, but they all seemed to adore Derek. Between his willingness to help with the barbecue to his different character impressions with the kids, he seemed to get along with everyone.

"So that's Derek, huh? Mr. I Love You?" Jazzy asked as she came into the kitchen. The two of them stood behind the island, staring at Derek playing with the kids in the living room.

"Yep, that's him." Taryn smiled despite herself.

"Not what I pictured as an actor," Jazzy confessed, tilting her head.

"Huh?" Taryn replied.

"Yeah, I think of actors and I think of these stuck-up Hollywood dudes that expect the world to just serve them, you know? He's just not that." Jazzy laughed.

"Nope. That doesn't sound like him at all. If I hadn't been to his set or seen his trailer, I don't think I would even believe he was an actor." Taryn giggled. "He's just Derek."

"Well, 'just Derek' is scoring a ton of brownie points with the family, just so you know." Jazzy winked.

"Thank goodness! That's one stress that I don't gotta worry about, I guess," Taryn replied.

"I do have a question though," Jazzy said cautiously. "What about Lewis?"

"What about him?" Taryn said with her brow furrowing.

"You know he has feelings for you, right?" Jazzy stated. "If he didn't, then he wouldn't have flown all the way out here to be with you through the Toby ordeal."

"We're just friends, Jaz. And he was just trying to make up for the ten years of not being there." Taryn scoffed.

"Or he lost you to Toby before, and when he finally found out you were single, he wasn't going to lose you again," Jazzy retorted.

"You're an idiot, you know that?" Taryn laughed nervously. "It's not like that with Lewis. Not anymore."

Frustrated, Jazzy shook her head and left her cousin in the kitchen, heading out to the backyard. Taryn slowly started to clean up, packing the leftover foods and washing the dishes.

"Can I help?" Derek whispered in her ear as he came up behind her.

"I'd appreciate that." Taryn smiled, turning and wrapping her arms around his waist. "You can start wiping these dishes."

"Yes, ma'am." He nodded, kissing her on her nose.

"Having fun with the kids, I see," Taryn said over her shoulder.

"Yeah!" Derek laughed. "I love kids. I think it's because I've always been one too," he added with a wink.

"You ready to go back to the Bay tomorrow?" Taryn sighed. "I'm kinda nervous."

"Well, after booking our tickets last night, since you canceled your other one," Derek began with a frown. "I'm glad you're *just* a little nervous. It seems as if you were avoiding coming back and probably wouldn't have if we weren't here to push you."

"In my defense, these last two weeks have been crazy. I canceled my original flight to go back to SF because I wasn't sure if I could go back that soon, with everything going on. But you're right. It did work out for the best that you guys came home. Now I don't gotta fly up by myself," Taryn admitted with a smile.

"Hello, Derek," Jazzy's voice interrupted. "So what's the deal with you and my lil sis here? I saw your text to her by the way, so just be straight with me, okay?"

"Jaz!" Taryn snapped.

"What? I want to see how he handles himself under pressure," Jazzy retorted with an evil smile.

"Yes, I told Taryn I love her, and yes, I meant it. I knew she was special from the moment I met her," Derek said with confidence, squaring his shoulders and standing tall.

Even if he looked as if he were holding his own, Taryn giggled to herself as his eyes hinted some fear toward Jazzy. The women in their family were all firecrackers, headstrong, blunt as hell, and sassy beyond measures. Jazzy was the most intimidating of them all.

"Didn't you, like, just meet her? It hasn't even been a month." Jazzy scoffed, crossing her arms. "And not to mention, majority of that time she's been in Hawai'i. So how do you know you love her? Because you're kinda sounding like a psycho right now."

Derek smiled and let out a slight laugh as he shook his head. Confusion spread across Jazzy's and Taryn's faces. Finally, Derek let out a long sigh.

"I know how crazy I sound. But when you know, you know. I told Taryn the night I got here that she had every right not to believe me. I also told her that I will prove it to her, and now I guess I'll just have to prove it to you too, Ms. Jazzy," Derek said.

"Good answer. But just know this. If you hurt her, even back in SF, it's going to be the last thing that you ever do. Okay? Have a great night," Jazzy threatened with a sarcastic smile as she walked away, leaving Taryn and Derek alone.

"Your cousin scares me," Derek whispered.

"That's Jazzy for you. You did good though. I'm actually impressed." Taryn smiled. "She made Toby cry and eat frog legs the first time she met him."

"That gives me hope then." Derek laughed.

"Hopefully." Taryn smirked as she headed to the backyard.

As the final family members left, Sienna and Tiana went about mopping and wiping the kitchen counters. Noah was taking out the trash as Derek helped Nathan collect the empty beer bottles. Taryn stood in the living room, folding the blankets the kids used for their nap, and she smiled as she looked at her family.

"Thank you, guys." She sighed, getting everyone's attention. "I know I don't talk much about everything. It's always been easier to keep it bottled inside. But having you guys here does mean a lot to me, and it has helped more than I could begin to explain."

"Of course, Ti! We're family. We got you," Sienna said.

"When I saw Marvin's body hanging, I felt like the biggest failure in the world. It was like his death symbolized not just me failing him but me failing at everything I was attempting in life. If I'm being honest, at one point, I felt like I should have been the one hanging from the end of the rope, you know?" Taryn confessed.

Tears filled up her eyes as she tried to explain herself. Everyone in the room froze, and all eyes fell onto her. This was the most honest she had been with them about her emotions in a long time, and none of them really knew how to act.

"Don't ever feel that way." Tiana finally broke her silence with a sob, walking over to her daughter.

"I can't help how I felt, Mom. But I do know that having all of you here with me made me not feel that way anymore. If it weren't for a support system like you guys, I don't think I would've made it past that night. So thank you," Taryn said.

They all dropped everything and drifted toward her, embracing Taryn in a huge group hug.

"We love you, Ti. We got you," Nathan emphasized.

Taryn nodded into their shoulders as they hugged it out, crying together. This was the first time Taryn had openly spoken with them about something she was going through in the past year, and it was a breakthrough, the start of her moving forward.

"Too much tears. Are you guys all packed already?" Noah asked, sniffling. "We'll wash clothes in the morning and dry them so you guys don't have any dirty ones to take back with you, okay?"

"Thanks, Dad," Taryn replied.

"Take care of each other in SF, all right?" Tiana sobbed. "Sienna, Derek? Watch out for our babies, okay?"

"We will," they chimed together.

"All right, off to bed. We can finish cleaning in the morning. Good night, guys," Noah said, pulling Tiana up the stairs.

"Good night," the four of them replied.

"Nate, you and Sienna head to bed. I can finish up down here." Taryn smiled.

"Thank you, Ti." Sienna sighed. "I'm exhausted."

"Good night, sis. Love you," Nathan said as they headed up the stairs.

They were alone at last. Derek pulled Taryn into his arms, planting a kiss gently on her lips. Then suddenly, he was kissing all over her face in a frenzy as she laughed. Staring into Derek's eyes, Taryn felt complete for the first time. It was as if despite everything going on, he was the glue that she needed to hold herself together.

"How about you jump in the shower, I'll finish up out here, and I'll meet you in ten minutes?" Taryn sighed, resting her chin on the hard apex of his chest.

"Or how about I help you finish up out here, and we can both go take a shower in five minutes?" Derek retorted, kissing her on the nose.

"Deal." She smiled.

37

Derek

The two of them finished wiping the counters, putting away the dishes, and mopping the floor with the Swifter before heading to Taryn's room. They locked the door behind them. Derek looked at Taryn lustfully. Even in ripped denim shorts, an old T-shirt, and her hair thrown up in a rubber band, unbrushed, she made his heart skip a beat and the blood in his body shoot straight to his groin.

Sitting on the love seat in the corner of her room, he waved her over. Slowly, she climbed onto his lap, straddling him with one leg on either side of his lean thighs. Relaxing into his lap, she could feel hardness growing in his shorts begin to push up against her bottom. Derek ran his hands up her thighs until they were resting on her round backside.

"Hi," she said innocently, draping her arms over his shoulders, locking her fingers together behind his neck.

"Hey." He smiled. "You ready to come back with me to the Bay tomorrow?"

"I'm not sure I'm ready to leave home. But with you by my side, I'm excited to be far from home this summer. I think at this point, it's very much needed. New beginnings, right?" She sighed.

"It's going to be a change, but a good one. And I promise I'll be by your side every step of the way, okay?" Derek reassured her, rubbing her back.

"Okay." Taryn sighed as she leaned forward and slipped her tongue past his lips.

"Nope," Derek said, pulling back, his chest heaving. "You had a long day, and we're traveling all day tomorrow. You need some rest."

"We can rest on the plane," Taryn retorted, rolling her eyes and grinding her hips onto his length.

"Ti, we'll have all summer together to do this," Derek groaned, motioning between the two of them with a wink. "Tonight, can you not use me for my body and just let me be with you?" he added jokingly.

"Okay. I'm sorry." Taryn laughed. "It's hard though. I think you got me addicted."

"Now you've taken it too far." Derek chuckled as he began to tickle Taryn's sides.

He didn't realize how ticklish she was, and it ended up sending her into a wiggling fit on his lap, causing the two of them to crash onto her bedroom floor in a laughing fit.

"Okay! Okay! I surrender!" Taryn choked out in broken breaths.

They lay intertwined in a mess of arms and legs. Derek laid there smiling as he stared at Taryn, the moonlight kissing her skin, making her glow.

"What?" she asked, noticing he was staring.

"Nothing." He sighed as he propped himself up on one elbow. "Everything just hits differently when you're in Hawai'i, huh? That or the more time I spend with you, the more I find myself falling in—"

"Derek, don't," Taryn interrupted, placing a finger gently on his lips. "You're crazy, you know that?"

"Crazy for what?" Derek asked as he gently squeezed her hand and removed it from his mouth. "Crazy for loving you?"

"Will you stop saying that?" Taryn exclaimed, standing up from the ground.

Derek was staring up at her with confusion. Pain suddenly filled her eyes, causing him to scramble off the floor in a panic. Was he wrong for telling her how he felt?

"Saying what? That I love you?" Derek asked, confused.

"Yes! I don't understand it!" Taryn began pacing across her bedroom floor.

"Understand what, Taryn? You're not making any sense. Why can't I say that I love you?" Derek said, his voice drenched in pain at the thought that she might not feel the same way, that her letter was just a fluke.

"BECAUSE! I DON'T LOVE MYSELF!" Taryn shouted as tears poured from her eyes, her chest heaving. "How could someone amazing like you love someone who can't even love herself? I'm damaged and broken. I'll never be good enough for you."

Derek's heart clenched in his chest. Everything Taryn had been through was impacting her more than anyone could ever realize. He loved her despite everything. Taryn was simply trying to push him away again. He walked over to her and cupped her face in his hands.

"Taryn, listen to me," he began, staring her in the eyes. "I love you. Damaged, broken, whatever it is. I love you and will always love you, no matter how crazy that sounds. I'm the one that's not good enough for someone brave, strong, and resilient like you. But that won't stop me from spending every breath I have in my lungs, to care for you and make you happy. I told you, I'm not going anywhere, so stop trying to push me away."

"But Derek—" Taryn began to argue.

"And if you don't love yourself, I'll love you enough for the both of us, okay? Now stop," Derek interrupted, pulling her into his chest. "I love you, Taryn."

On a huff, Taryn conceded and melted into his arms. After a quick shower, the two of them climbed into bed, the exhaustion from the day catching up to them. Despite being so tired, Derek couldn't sleep. He kept looking over at the woman next to him, wondering how someone with such a big heart had no room in it to love herself. In that moment, he made it his goal to fill her with love every chance he got this summer. Plans for their summer began to occupy his mind, and before he knew it, he was dreaming of Taryn with him in the Bay as sleep finally took him.

38

Taryn

The airport was unusually crowded. Tiana and Noah pulled the 4Runner up to the curb as Taryn, Nathan, Sienna, and Derek got out. As the men unloaded the bags from the trunk, Tiana began to say her goodbyes.

"Thank you so much, Mom," Taryn said with a heavy sigh. With everything she had been through this year, especially within the last month, words couldn't begin to describe how much it meant to her that her parents allowed her to cope according to her own timetable, not pushing for answers but being the first there to extend a hug when she was ready.

"Of course," Tiana said, her voice breaking, knowing her daughter was thanking her for more than just the ride to the airport.

"We'll see you in July!" Sienna exclaimed excitedly. As a late Mother's Day and Father's Day gift, the kids split the cost to fly Tiana and Noah up to spend the Fourth of July weekend with them in the Bay.

"Yes, we'll see you guys. It'll give us a break from the summer heat," Noah replied as he pulled the final bag onto the curb next to Taryn. "Watch out for our girl, okay, Derek?"

"Yes, sir," Derek agreed, shaking Noah's hand.

"Okay, we gotta go. Love you guys!" Nathan said as he gave his parents a final hug.

"Love you guys!" Tiana replied as they got in the car, waving as they pulled away from the curb.

The hustle and bustle of the airport kept things lively, occupying Taryn's mind as they went through the motions to check-in. Again, since it was a last-minute booking, all they had left was first class. Derek had argued to pay for all four of them, but Taryn went into older sister mode. She refused to let him, and they ended up coming to the compromised agreement that he could pay for her ticket, but she was going to pay for Sienna and Nathan's since he had already paid for them to come home. With the first-class priority, a Hawaiian Airlines worker took their bags from them, and they skipped the line at TSA. It was a dream.

"Yep, never gonna be able to fly coach again. Thanks a lot, assholes," Nathan scoffed jokingly as they headed to their terminal.

"What he means to say is thank you, guys. And once we start making the big bucks, we owe you two a first-class trip to go skiing in Canada or something." Sienna laughed.

"Anytime," Taryn said. "Thank you, guys, for coming home for me."

"Anytime," Derek replied with a wink.

As the boys settled in at the terminal, the girls headed to the bathroom to relieve themselves one last time before boarding started in fifteen minutes.

"So you and Derek, huh?" Sienna smiled.

"I guess." Taryn giggled nervously. "I'm not sure what it is, but I feel happy when I'm around him. Do you think it's too soon?"

"Girl! It's not soon enough!" Sienna exclaimed. "You deserve to be happy, Ti. You're always trying to make everyone else around you happy. Now that we're all okay, you need to think about yourself. So if he makes you happy, just go with it."

"You're absolutely right. I guess I was so focused on making sure everyone else was happy that I forgot what it felt like to be happy myself." Taryn sighed.

"Well, if he's what makes you happy, be selfish!" She smiled.

"Thanks, Sienna. You're truly the little sister I never had!" Taryn embraced Sienna. Suddenly, pungent smells of the bathroom invaded Taryn's nose, and she staggered backward, gripping the sink.

"Ti, you okay?" Sienna was worried.

"I… I, um…" Before Taryn could finish her sentence, she felt the bile rise in her throat and the sour spit filled the corners of her mouth as she sprinted for the nearest toilet bowl. It was as if her guts came spewing out of her mouth as it hit the water with an awful sound.

"Ti!" Sienna was kneeling at her side, holding her hair back in an instant. Rubbing her back with her other hand, she stared in horror as Taryn's entire body heaved, vomit pouring from her mouth in waterfalls. "Are you okay? What the fuck?"

Finally catching her breath, Taryn took some toilet paper and wiped the corners of her mouth before tossing it in and flushing. She was gasping for air as she slumped to the floor, leaning against the stall wall.

"What the fuck was that?" Sienna asked, eyes wide.

"I don't know. It must've been something I ate." Taryn tried to think back.

"We all ate pretty much the same thing for breakfast. What did you eat at Zippy's?" Sienna reasoned.

"The only thing different that I had was the hamburger steak. You guys all ate the Korean fried chicken, and we all had some mac salad and fries. So maybe it was the gravy? Maybe it was spoiled or something." Taryn's breathing began to return to normal.

"Well, whatever it was, it did not sit well with you, girl. Come on. Let's go rinse your mouth. It kinda reeks now," Sienna said jokingly.

As the two women pulled themselves from the ground, Sienna placed an arm around Taryn's waist to steady her. Taryn continued to take deep breaths as they headed over to the sink. Sienna wet some napkins and offered them to Taryn to clean herself up a bit more. After rinsing her mouth, she gratefully took a piece of gum from Sienna.

"You ready?" Sienna asked.

"I think so." Taryn smiled as they headed from the bathroom.

The cool air of the airport helped to dry the cold sweat that had formed on Taryn's forehead as they walked. Color began to return to Taryn's cheeks just as they got back to the terminal in time to board.

"We will now be boarding first-class passengers for Flight HA58 with service to San Francisco. Please have your boarding pass ready," the announcer said over the loudspeaker.

"You two okay?" Nathan asked with a frown as Taryn and Sienna approached.

"We're fine." Taryn smiled, grabbing her bag as Derek stood up next to her.

"Ready?" Sienna gave Taryn a questioning look.

Taryn simply smiled, and Sienna realized that she didn't want to freak Nathan out by telling him she was feeling sick. So Sienna kept quiet and nodded her agreement.

"You guys are weird. But okay then. Let's go." Nathan sighed, grabbing his bags and leading the way with Sienna following close behind him.

"Let me get your bag," Derek said, taking the handle to Taryn's rolling carry-on and following behind Sienna.

Just as they were standing in line to scan their boarding passes, Taryn's phone buzzed in her purse. A new text message popped up on her screen.

"Can't wait to spend some time with you this summer! Miss you a lot already. See you in class when you get here, Professor." (Lewis)

"Ti, you coming?" Derek turned to her with a smile as he waited for her on the jetway.

"Sorry. I was just checking my phone. I thought someone was calling." Taryn smiled. "It was nothing."

Shoving her phone back into her bag, she looked at Derek towering gorgeously in front of her. She could see his muscles flexing with every movement through his long sleeve shirt, generating that burning desire inside of her just by looking at him. Taryn sighed to herself. Man, was this going to be a long summer. She was eager to find out what the future had to hold for her and Derek. But at the same time, she couldn't rid herself of this nagging feeling of the what-ifs with Lewis. Could they really just be friends? She didn't want to hurt him. But the real question was, who was her heart calling out to more? Only the summer could tell. As she walked down the long hall toward the entrance to the plane, Taryn wasn't just walking toward her summer. She was walking toward events that would test her strength, question her beliefs, and suddenly change the course of her future forever.

ABOUT THE AUTHOR

 *Shattered* is the second novel in the *Fallen* series written by Gianna Emiko Barnes. The novels were written as brain breaks while she was finishing her dissertation writing for her doctorate degree. She used fictional writing as an escape from the stress of the real world. Her day job as an English teacher has solidified a deep-set love for writing that has always been a passion of Gianna's, allowing her a safe outlet for healing when going through various heartaches and losses throughout her life.

In her writing, she loves to portray realistic characters and storylines that are often inspired by actual experiences and people who have impacted her life. The values of loyalty, respect, and family are also emphasized in her novels as they were key components in her upbringing in Hawai'i. Despite the obstacles her characters face and overcome in order to grow as individuals throughout her novels, Gianna also emphasizes, time and time again, the importance of staying true to yourself. She hopes that through the realistic approaches to her writing, readers can gain a sense of hope, comfort, and support in knowing that regardless if the storyline is fictional, they, too, can learn to overcome any obstacle in life and find happiness.

CPSIA information can be obtained
at www.ICGtesting.com
Printed in the USA
LVHW020500130821
695223LV00010B/858